The
Mystery of
Sneaky Paws

Pam Kumpe

Pam Kumpe

DEDICATION

For the muddy, the lonely, and the orphan.

Pam Kumpe

Fear not, for I am with you; be not dismayed, for I am your
God; I will strengthen you, I will help you, I will
uphold you with my righteous hand.
Isaiah 41:10 ESV

I will not leave you as orphans. I will come to you.
John 14:18 ESV

DISCLAIMER

Custard

THE MUDDY CHASE

My name's Emma Hobbit, and I have a new story for you. It's about a scrappy, yellow dog, Custard, a bunch of us kids, and a big spooky adventure to an old house two blocks from my street, close to the woods, right next to the interstate in Lick Skillet. But let's rewind to the start, to where it all began—on Christmas break.

Passing sixth grade is my top mission—well, it should be, but I have this knack for finding things, especially things that aren't looking to be found. So I jump into action, and, without a second thought, my homework gets shoved to the back burner or slips my mind entirely. But lately, there's been one thing, or should I say one wagging tail, that's got my attention: Custard. Why does he always dash off to the creepy, abandoned Mitchell house?

And there's another thing that's looping through my mind like a stuck video—it's a news story about a kid my age who survived a nasty car wreck on the interstate a couple of weeks ago.

Also, here's something else you should know; my little brother Brett went to heaven nearly five years ago, after a terrible accident from our treehouse. Losing him ripped a big hole in my heart, and then in October, on the camping trip with our youth group, I nearly lost Brett's stuffed elephant. That scare woke something up inside me. So losing Custard, the rescue dog I found at school–it's unthinkable. He found me. And I need him.

After the camping trip, my friend Sebastian Wisconsin thanked me a million times for reuniting him with his grandpa, and since then, he appointed himself as my tutor to improve my grades and pay me back. He doesn't owe me anything, but I've learned that trying to stop Sebastian is like trying to stop the rain on a stormy day. With so many math and history tests and newfound popularity, my packed schedule doesn't allow much time for homework. Or that's what I keep saying.

Of course, the risk of not passing the sixth grade makes me cringe when I think about it. My dad thinks Custard is a considerable part of the recent problem with my lack of focus, so he makes sure I keep pinning up posters in hopes someone would claim a missing dog. But I keep praying that each poster gets blown away and that no one comes for Custard.

Jack Cleverton, one of my best friends, is no help, either, because he told Sebastian I create chaos out of nothing, which is true in some sense. He suggested Custard go to the shelter, but no one was sending my dog to a lonely cage in a cold building. I'm this dog's new master—after all, he licked my face a hundred times on the ride home from school that day.

Now, nearly sixty days of bonding are behind us, and the longer Custard stays, the odds of his living with me get better.

It's the first Monday of Christmas break. So Mom and I ran an errand for wrapping paper. As she drove the SUV downtown, I gazed out the passenger window, and many of the flyers still flapped from poles. A few were gone, and I accidentally pulled one off a store's window when no one looked and tossed the flyer into a trash can.

On that same window hung a flyer with a photo of a 12-year-old boy with black curly hair and dark eyes who may have survived the recent car crash—on the interstate. The reporter who wrote a newspaper story said the boy never surfaced from the wreckage, although some believed he was never in the car—but no one knows.

9

As I wrestled to get comfortable in the front seat of our SUV after tossing sparkly green wrapping paper into the back, I wiped a tear from my cheek—the idea of a boy without his parents at Christmas was too much to think about. I stared at the Christmas lights in the windows at the beauty shop, the pharmacy, and the restaurant known for home-style cooking while Mom drove around the corner, heading home.

Mom interrupted my daydreaming. "Emma, we're not planning on keeping Custard. You know that?"

Sighing, I nodded, her words a reminder that I must work on letting Custard lick her face more often—to sway her. "Yes, ma'am," I responded, confident I meant it but hoping I didn't.

I blew on the window beside me, creating a fog on the glass, and I scribbled Custard's name with my finger. "Mom, do you think a lost boy is hiding in our town?" I didn't wait for her to answer and said, "I don't think it's possible. No one could have survived that wreck. The newspaper story included a photo that showed what was left of the car. It was beyond burnt."

Mom clutched the steering wheel. "There's talk that the boy might have died with his parents in the fire, but so far, no one knows if that's true. Either way, the whole thing is so tragic. And here it is, nearly Christmas."

I let out all the air in my lungs. "I don't think I'll ever get my driver's license. Too many terrible things happen in cars. I never want to drive."

"Emma Hobbit, I promise. You'll want to drive like every other teenager. And you'll beg me for a car, too. But first, we've got to raise your grades so you can make it to seventh grade next year."

I ignored her comment about my grades. "I enjoy walking. It's safer." I circled Custard's name on the glass with a heart.

"Emma. That's how you feel now, and we both know how fast you change your mind and regret what you say."

As the engine hummed, my thoughts focused on Custard, my heart heavy at the idea of giving him up to someone else. But so far, no one has called, unless you count the one lady who described a fuzzy, black, fifty-pound dog. She couldn't have looked at Custard's photo on the poster because he weighed twelve pounds and had golden yellow hair and floppy ears. As for his breed, he's simply a mix of perfection and cuteness.

Custard may have dug his way into my life, but he's escaped from the backyard more than a dozen times. He's a little bundle of energy with a knack for trouble, and he goes to the old Mitchell house every time he gets free. Dad believes he's meant for the yard and borrowed a doghouse, which Custard stands on and howls. But I think he's hollowing because our neighbor, Jane Hendershot, plays her guitar on the porch—she's lonely and pushing fifty-something—and he's singing for her.

Custard's meant for the inside of our house, mainly so he can sleep with me—no howling involved.

Mom and Dad are both on edge about Custard, but they don't like to watch me cry—which I can do with little thought—so maybe a few extra tears will let Custard stay longer.

Today, after we shopped, Custard decided another escape from the backyard might add to the excitement, and since the winter rain had softened the dirt by the fence, he was out before I knew it. Mom cornered him by Jane's driveway between our houses, and when I caught up to Mom, the mud from Custard's paws coated her clothes and face. Bath time was inevitable for Custard.

Jane moved toward the excitement. "Emma, your little pup is the cutest thing, even when he howls in the yard." She wiped a few splats of mud from her face with her sleeve. "I've got to find a song that helps him sing in tune, though."

Holding Custard as he squirmed, I said, "His ears must hurt when you play the guitar."

Mom tugged on my arm. "Emma means she's sure Custard's ears are sensitive."

"I understand. My music isn't for everyone."

I nodded. "That's what I meant," and carried Custard into the house, taking him promptly to the bathroom. Leaning over the tub, I declared, "Custard, you're getting a scrubbing whether or not you like it," but he just wagged his three-inch tail, oblivious to my pretending to be annoyed.

I scrubbed his paws and couldn't help but think about how Mom says my middle name should be Rescue since I do that with anything that seems lost. As I was about to scrub his ear, the doorbell rang, and I heard Mom answer the door. "Come in. She's giving Custard another bath."

My brainy classmate, Sebastian, who loved reading, math, and everything historical, pounded my way. "Hey, Emma.

13

You missed our appointment at the library. I'm supposed to tutor you during Christmas break, but you missed our first meeting. Is everything okay?" Sebastian hovered by the bathroom door, peeking inside, and added, "Your mom let me in."

Before I could answer, Custard, seizing the opportunity, bolted from my arms. A wild chase ensued, with Custard leaving a trail of muddy footprints in his wake. Ever the gentleman, Sebastian tried to catch him, but Custard was a blur of mischief and splats of dirty soapy water.

During the commotion, the doorbell chimed again. Jack, panting and anxious, met us in the hallway. "Guys, I need your help. My drone's caught in a branch in the Mitchell's tree in the backyard."

"One second," I called, peeking into Mom's bedroom and back. "I've got Custard cornered in here. He's on the bed."

Mom tore past me. "My bed! The comforter is filthy!" She jumped around the mattress in sync with Custard and put her hands on her hips. Trailing her, Jack put his arms on his hips, too, and Sebastian and I waved our arms, our steps closing in, and I snatched up Custard. "Gotcha!"

Jack brought the conversation back to his lost drone. "Remember the Mitchell house, the two-story off Maple Street?"

Hurrying to the bathroom, I said, "Yeah, that's where Melvin and Joyce lived before the pandemic got them. It's a creepy place, wrapped in rumors and mystery. It's where Custard goes whenever he escapes."

"I remember how the Mitchells kept to themselves unless we saw them at church. They weren't that old, but now they're gone. And the house has been for sale for years." Jack rubbed Custard's ear.

"Let me finish with Custard's bath, and I'll go with you. So will Sebastian."

Sebastian sighed, "Sure. It's not like we're doing any studying today."

"We'll study tomorrow," I said, assuring Sebastian.

Jack smiled, blocking the door—to keep Custard in the bathroom. "Custard, you get into too much trouble. You need to take an obedience class."

Sebastian moved to the other end of the tub, where he picked up a bottle of dog shampoo. "Emma and Custard both could stand to take an obedience class, but mostly, Emma. She missed her first tutoring session this morning. I've volunteered to help her with history and math—so she can raise her grades. And she never showed."

I bumped into him with my shoulder. "Stop. I've got pressing things to do. I just forgot!"

"We talked early this morning. How could you forget so soon?"

"I went with Mom to the store. I thought that might be more fun than learning." I hovered over the tub. "Come on, Custard. Time for that bath!"

Jack reminded me to hurry. "Get that dog clean. We've got to get my drone. My dad permitted me to open one present in advance, specifically for use during the holiday. And it was a drone! But I'm not great with the controls yet."

"Let me finish washing, Custard, and I'll go with you."

Sebastian took a stab at me. "We still have time for history and math."

"Not today; we have bigger things to do."

Mom added her two cents when she peeked into the bathroom. "Remember, Custard left muddy footprints all over my bedspread. You'll need to take care of that, too."

"Yes, ma'am." I rubbed the shampoo over Custard's back and soaped up legs using a scrubby. "I've got to finish cleaning this puppy and take care of Mom's bedspread, then we'll rescue your drone," I told Jack, eyeing the muddy paw prints on the floor.

Sebastian sighed. "Fine, I'll help with the drone search, too. There might be some great history hiding in that old house."

We worked together, laughing and joking, trying to make the best of the situation, and with Jack and Sebastian's help, the mud was soon gone, the floor clean, and Mom's bedspread swished in the washer.

The bath had included a battle of slippery paws, and I reminded Custard to behave when I rinsed him off—which brought Sebastian's reminder that I could learn from my own words. But eventually, Custard emerged, slightly less muddy, and looked rather pleased with himself. With a quick towel dry, he was ready for his next adventure, although he didn't know it yet.

Finally, the house was in order. "Time to go drone-hunting," I announced, feeling excitement and apprehension.

We stepped outside, the chilly air biting at our cheeks. That's when disaster struck. Custard darted out ahead through the opened door, a streak of speed and determination.

"Not again!" I yelled, my heart dropping. "You just had a bath."

Sebastian said, "Obedience school for Custard shouldn't be an option—it should be mandatory."

I charged down the street. "Custard! Wait up!"

Sebastian

EERIE EYES AND DARK SHADOWS

The chase was on with Custard in the lead. This became the umpteenth time he'd run off. "Custard, you better stop," I yelled.

Sebastian panted, "Why do I always run when I'm with you, Emma?"

Jack patted Sebastian on the back, sprinting ahead. "Running is great. It keeps us in shape."

"I'm not planning on being on the track team."

I laughed. "Yes, you are. We're on track to catch a dog."

Jack reminded me. "… and to retrieve a drone."

The three of us dashed to the corner, calling Custard by name, but he was on a mission to explore or enjoy the thrill of the hunt. We followed him around the next street, past curious neighbors and barking dogs, until we stood in front of the old Mitchell house—where the for-sale sign sported black spray paint with the word *haunted* painted on it.

The drone was the last thing on my mind, as Custard caught my attention in the muddy driveway. His trail led me to the front of the house, where he always stopped to sniff the old wooden swing at the end of the porch before darting to the backyard.

I marched, clapping my hands, and called Custard. "Come on, boy. Come to Emma." The two-story house loomed over us, its windows dark, as if empty eyes peered at us from the windows upstairs. "Did you see that? I saw a shadow."

Jack argued. "You're always seeing things. I need to find my drone."

Sebastian rubbed his hands together, cracking his knuckles. "I want to see inside that house. Shadows lead to history. And history is important. We've never gone inside before; let's go."

I waved my arms. "Yeah, it's calling to us. But first, I've got to catch Custard. He's not on the porch anymore."

Jack pointed. "There he goes. He's headed to the back."

I yelled, "Custard Hobbit! Stop!"

Sebastian asked, "You've given him your last name?"

"You have a last name. He deserves one, too."

"Guys, I know my drone's back there in the tree. We can get Custard and my drone," Jack said.

A part of me, the curious, adventurous girl, wanted to see what secrets the house kept inside its walls, but first, I had to retrieve my dog. "Custard!" I called, but he was already gone, and the three of us rounded the back of the house, stopping in our tracks when the back door on the small porch creaked with an eerie moan.

We exchanged glances—the moment of decision. With a deep breath, I stepped forward, with Sebastian and Jack by my side. "We're in this together; come on, you two. The door is open."

Casting a glance at us, Custard swiftly disappeared into the shadows inside while Jack confidently headed to the Oak tree. "I'm after my drone. It's up there. I'll join you two in a few minutes."

"Then it's just you and me, Sebastian." We trooped inside the dark and dusty house, the corners filled with silhouettes from the furniture, but mostly silence. We moved cautiously, and Sebastian held a flashlight. "Where in the world did you get that?" I asked, shocked he came prepared.

"It was on the kitchen counter when we came inside. I figured it might come in handy." Sebastian grinned, his eyes gleaming with confidence.

"I'm surprised the batteries work." I shrugged my shoulders, letting that thought drop like a cobweb cut loose by the wind of doubt.

Every creak on the floor and groan from the walls made us jump, but we pressed on, determined to find Custard. "Here, boy. Come to Emma. You're not in trouble."

As we explored, Sebastian and I discovered remnants of the life of Melvin and Joyce. Pictures were on the walls, an old piano in the corner, a cozy armchair with a knitting basket beside it. And lots of dust. It was sad to see all the things left behind.

We circled the hallway that made a loop and discovered Custard back in the kitchen, his nose buried in an old, empty dog bowl. "Stay right where you are. I've got you."

He looked up, his tail wagging, as if to say, "What took you so long?"

Sebastian peered out the kitchen window, the dingy-dusty curtains waving like they, too, held secrets. "Jack's climbing down from the tree, but I don't see the drone in his hand. Now, he's next to the bushes by the alley. He must have knocked the drone to the ground. Wait, he's behind the garage. Where is he going?"

Then, like a cat caught in a lawnmower's blade, a scream pierced the air, and I grabbed Sebastian's arm. "Did you hear that?" I moved closer to his side as I cradled Custard in my arms. Sebastian whispered, "What was that?"

Custard wiggled, dove from my grasp, and took off from the kitchen, darting into the hallway—toward the cat's cry. I ran after him, but he swiftly bounced up the stairs and slid into the darkness.

I stood at the bottom of the staircase, and a wisp of air made my hair dance as if a window had opened upstairs, letting the cold air fly inside. "Custard's after a cat, I'm sure of it. But it's so much darker up there than down here. And eerier." I held the knob on the rail, and it fell from my hand, clacking like thunder to the floor. Unsure if I could muster up the guts to go up the stairs, I placed the knob back onto the rail.

Sebastian's voice quivered from behind me. "I'll go check on Jack. He probably needs my help."

I turned to him. "Seriously, you're deserting a poor little girl when she needs you. What about your history search? You said Jack left, remember?"

"Trust me. You're braver than me. And tougher." And with that, Sebastian darted from my side, but not before he shoved the flashlight into my hand.

I experienced a chilling sensation as I moved forward. The house wasn't just an empty shell; it was a keeper of stories, and for a moment, I became a part of its newest history—the part of the story where I'd most likely scream like a baby.

Custard materialized at the top of the stairs, his ears straight back, and he dove toward me, sailing in the air so fast he nearly knocked me over at the bottom of the staircase. "Custard, you've got to learn to obey. You can't keep running off," I said as my words echoed up and down the stairs like a whirlwind. I turned to gaze up the stairs, hoping the stray cat would show himself. But nothing. Just silence.

Custard and I emerged into the daylight in the backyard, a little happier for the sunlight, and I'd placed the flashlight on the counter where Sebastian first found it to ensure I took nothing that wasn't mine. Custard trotted beside me, his adventure-driven curiosity momentarily satisfied, his loyalty unfolding with a token of obedience.

As I walked across the yard, Sebastian held his hands out. "Well, Jack's truly gone. It seems like he found his drone and left us. He's nowhere to be found."

I wiped a spider web from my shirt. "As you can see, I'm fine, too. No monsters got me." I looked around. "That's not like Jack. He doesn't leave without telling me. Are you sure he's gone?"

"Do you see him? I'm not blind." Sebastian spun like a top, emphasizing, "See, it's you, me, and Custard. Jack went home."

I nodded, knowing I was the last to understand boys, dogs, or drones. My friendship with Jack and Sebastian is much like pursuing a naughty dog. It's unpredictable, sometimes messy, but always an adventure worth taking. And sometimes, you hear screams and then need to go home.

As for the Mitchell house, that's a story for another day. Jack had his drone, and I had Custard walking beside me as if he'd never run off.

Sebastian said, "I'm going back to the library." He stopped a few feet away and turned back, offering one last plea. "This is our first Monday on Christmas break. If you want to get better grades, you must apply yourself. We could get in a few minutes of studying."

"Not today. I will apply myself—like tomorrow."

The blue sky wiped away the remaining gray clouds, casting a warm, golden light over Lick Skillet. The warmth felt like a sign, a promise of brighter days to come. Custard was calm and obedient, and every few steps, he nudged my leg with his nose, and then Mom showed up at the front door as I stepped onto our porch. "Emma, how many detergent pods did you drop into the washing machine?"

I tore into the house, rushing to the laundry room, where a mound of bubbles met me. Custard slid in behind me, like skating on thin ice—which, in some ways, might be true.

"Let me think. I put ten pods into the washer before I left. Custard got your bedspread super muddy. Was that too much?"

On the slippery tile, Mom shook her head, balancing herself with outstretched hands on each side of the narrow entrance, and Custard swiftly darted between her legs, suggesting it was time for a nap—a time for him to hide.

Mom blew air from her pursed lips. "Emma, Custard is a lot of work. It may be time for us to chat about where he lives—and it might not be here. And you need a few laundry lessons, too."

"Wait, you don't give up on me when I mess up. You believe in me. You give me chances to do better. Custard is family now. You can't abandon him. He needs me."

The washing machine rattled, dancing like an overloaded soap dispenser, and I slipped to the floor. And so did Mom.

"Mom, did you hurt yourself?"

"No! But your escapades and that of Custard seem to grow faster than we can keep this house clean," she said, wiping suds from her brow.

Then, from behind her as she sat on the tile, Custard inched up, licking her face as if she tasted like a cinnamon taffy.

"Look, Custard is saying he's sorry."

"If he keeps running away and escaping from the backyard and darting out the front door, we will have to find him a permanent home—elsewhere, like the dog shelter."

Custard whined as if he understood, and I rubbed his ear. "Mom didn't mean it. She won't give up on you. You'll see."

In seconds, Dad came in from work, calling for us. "Where is everyone? I've brought pizza!" He marched our way, but before we could tell him to stop, to warn him of the excess suds and water, Custard jumped at Dad. He knocked the pizza box from Dad's hand—and the box flew open, tossing a Frisbee of pizza slices our way.

Mom straddled the suds and pizza sauce. "Today's been one of those days!"

I gulped. "Hi, Dad. You can take that out of my allowance."

Dad shook his head and mentioned, "You don't get an allowance right now. Remember, you're using your allowance for dog food until Custard's rightful owner claims him."

"Oh, yeah." I sighed, hugging my dad, smiling at my mom, and wishing Custard knew how to apologize for being so unruly.

Dad helped Mom into the kitchen and turned to remind me. "We've got to decide. Custard is becoming way too much trouble. So, I'm not sure what we'll end up doing. How did your tutoring go today with Sebastian?"

My shoulders slumped. "I went shopping with Mom, and then Custard escaped. And Jack's drone landed in a tree. The day got away."

Dad snorted from both nostrils with a whistle. "Custard, what are we going to do with you?"

Emma & Harper

SHADOWS AND WHISPERS

I spent the next two hours swooshing suds into the backyard with a broom, and now I positioned the clean bedspread, smoothing it out on Mom's bed, and Custard sat by my feet as I smoothed the wrinkles. "Stay off this bed. If you keep acting up, Mom and Dad will follow through on their threat. So, behave, and don't give them a reason to send you away."

Custard stretched, propping his front feet onto the side of the bed, and nudged my hand with his black nose as if to say he knew what my words meant.

Mom's cell phone sent a shrill ring through the house, piercing the evening's calm, the noise pulling me away from petting Custard. I headed to the living room, and Mom answered her cell with a worried frown. "Hello? Mr. Cleverton. No, Jack's not here. He stopped by earlier, but he left with Emma hours ago." Mom paused, then said, "Yes, Emma's here."

I spoke up. "Remember, we went to the Mitchell house searching for his drone? That's when Custard charged out the door. But I haven't seen him since." I danced around Mom, rattling off information like Mr. Cleverton could hear me.

Mom repeated my words to Jack's dad. "Emma reminded me he'd lost his drone in a tree at the Mitchell house. And Sebastian and Emma searched with him." Mom paused, listening, and said, "I'm sure he's fine. He'll be home soon."

I felt a knot form in my stomach. "Mom, Jack doesn't just disappear. Besides, Mr. Cleverton surprised Jack with the drone after church yesterday, even though Christmas is a week away. Jack wouldn't wander off. That's not like him."

Mom ended the call, turning to me. "Emma, seriously, you're rattling on and on, and listening to both of you isn't easy. Mr. Cleverton is worried because he's called Jack's phone, but no answer. Are you sure you saw Jack leave for home?"

"I'm sure he left the Mitchell house after he found his drone." I scratched my head, unsure if I was speaking the complete truth. "Maybe he went to the library. I know that's where Sebastian went. I bet he's fine."

Mom moved to the window and glanced at the street. "I hope he's all right. But why wouldn't he answer his phone?"

Scratching my head, I knew what I had to do. "I'm going back to the Mitchell house. He might have gone back. Maybe he dropped his phone in the yard and went to retrieve it," I said with determination.

I put Custard on a leash, took off to Maple Street, and slogged back toward the old Mitchell House. The air was colder now, the sky a dull gray, with new clouds floating overhead as if mirroring my worry. I reminded Custard. "Mom made me promise to come right back, not to be gone for over thirty minutes, or else."

As I approached the Mitchell's backyard, a voice called out from the back gate. "Emma? Is that you?" I rushed to a familiar face in the alley. "Harper Hensley! Are you visiting your grandparents for Christmas?"

"Yes, you know, they live right behind this old house. I just arrived today and saw you and a boy I didn't know. And this little guy." Harper bent down and petted Custard's head. "He's the cutest dog ever."

"His name is Custard. I found him at school a couple of months ago. And so far, no one's claimed him. So he's living with me."

"Oh, the poor thing. He's an orphan."

"He's not an orphan now. I've adopted him. I'm his new family."

Harper danced around Custard. "So when I saw you from the upstairs window of my grandma's house, I saw Jack in a tree, too."

I hugged Harper's neck. "He was after his drone. Gosh, I'm so glad to see you. Did you see which way Jack went? His dad is looking for him. I came back here in case he came back this way."

Harper twirled in her camouflage sweats and gray jacket, her curly brown hair like a rope twisted together in threads. "He left down the alley. But wait, he returned right after you and that other kid left." Harper sighed. "So, who's the new boy?"

"That's Sebastian Wisconsin. He's in the sixth grade with me. He moved here during the summer before school started." I swallowed hard. "Gosh, I wish you still lived here. Since you moved away to Arkansas, I only see you at Christmas and sometimes in the summer."

"I wish we could move back. School is lonely without you. You make school fun."

Smiling, I said, "Cinnamon taffy helps too." I reached into my pocket. "Here, I always keep cinnamon taffy for moments like this."

"Thanks, I haven't had taffy in forever."

I stepped toward the bushes by the alley next to the garage. "Jack's not answering his cell phone. I wonder if he dropped it in the yard." I paraded around the tree and the hedge and glanced under the bushes.

Harper danced around Custard again. "Last, I remember Jack stuck his head inside the house through the back door, now that I think about it. Maybe he went inside." She smoothed her hoodie, unwrapping a piece of taffy, and tossed it into her mouth—and I glanced at my navy-blue hoodie— same as hers, but a different color.

I circled back over my steps. "It's possible that Jack picked up on the meow from the cat inside the house. And we all know that Jack loves cats." The sun slid behind another cloud, and I knew my thirty minutes ticked faster with each breath. "I sure have missed you, Harper."

"I've missed you too. We must spend every free minute together over Christmas break."

"I have to take tutoring daily, but we'll make time."

"Why do you need a tutor?"

"My grades have slipped. I've got to raise them or repeat sixth grade."

Harper shook me with both hands, holding my shoulders. "Wait, you're smarter than most of us. What's wrong?"

"Nothing's wrong. I'm just not into school."

"Hey, we're going to college together one day. It would be best if you tried harder. I don't want to go alone."

"College? I'm just trying to graduate from middle school someday."

We laughed and ventured toward the back door together, but I turned and trooped to the tree to check for Jack's phone on the ground again.

Harper yelled, "Emma, look!" She pointed to the upstairs window, and a shadow peered at us from behind the thin curtain. We both froze; the figure stared back but then disappeared.

I inched toward Harper, grabbing her hand. "It could be Jack!"

"But he knows us. He wouldn't hide," Harper said, and without thinking, we both rushed to the house, the door creaking as I pushed it open. "Jack? Are you upstairs?" I called out, but the only answer was an echo of my voice bouncing off the walls.

Harper and I searched, tiptoeing, our steps cautious and quiet. Then, a figure darted past us from the shadow by the stairs and soared outside through the kitchen door. It was a boy, about our age, but not Jack. He ran with a desperation that spoke of fear and urgency, and we rushed after him as if that were our only option. But the boy slid into the woods beside the house, which led nowhere except toward the interstate.

Harper and I stopped running when he faded into the thick, tall trees bordering the property. Panting and out of breath, I suddenly had a realization. "That boy, I have seen his face before," I said, my mind racing.

Harper wiped her brow. "So, he's new in town, too?" She bent down, petting Custard, whose tongue hung out from all the chasing.

I rubbed my nose. "I think we were running after the kid from the car accident. In town, there are posters about a boy who's been missing after his parents' wreck on the interstate. Their car caught fire, and the man and woman died."

Harper sighed, her mouth wide open. "What? How horrible!"

"It was all over the news. Some people thought the boy had died in the flames, but others heard he'd escaped. The wreck happened a couple of weeks back. Maybe he survived?"

Harper and I exchanged a look of disbelief. "We must find him, Emma. He might need our help," she said, her voice firm.

Despite its shadows, the Mitchell house appeared to be at the heart of another Emma Hobbit investigation. "We're going to need help in finding the boy," I said, gripping Custard's leash.

Harper asked, "But what about Jack?"

"Let's make sure Jack's not here, and then we'll get help for the boy."

Harper zipped up her hoodie. "But we better hurry. That boy is all alone, if you're right."

We hurried across the backyard, tore through the kitchen, and stopped at the bottom of the staircase. "Earlier, Custard chased something, and I thought it was a cat; maybe the boy made those noises to distract us." I wiped the hair from my face. "But it can't be. I distinctly heard a cat meowing."

"What, exactly, are you looking for?" Harper asked.

"Clues. Something to point us in the right direction. And, of course, Jack."

We climbed the stairs, and I couldn't shake the feeling of being watched. The photographs on the wall at the top of the second floor seemed to follow our every move. "Harper, the secrets within this house are longing to be discovered. Look at this photo. It's Jane, my neighbor. She's standing with Joyce Mitchell. I didn't know they were friends." I ran my fingers around the outline of my neighbor's face.

Harper touched the photo. "I bet they were the best of friends. Both were a lot younger in this photo." She clapped her hands like she did when ready for an adventure. "Let's split up. You check that room, and I'll check this one over here," she said.

I nodded, the weight of the situation settling on my shoulders, and Custard followed me on his leash, his ears twisting in every direction.

At the top of the stairs, I pushed the door open; the floor creaked under my weight, adding to the unanswered groans that seemed to fill the house. "Jack? Are you here? I know you returned after you left, and I need to rule out whether you're inside this house. Don't be playing; answer me if you're here." I called out again, my voice barely a whisper.

Room by room, we searched, and dust specks danced in the shafts of light that pierced through the gloom, the surrounding silence almost suffocating. "Harper, I don't think Jack is here. We better go."

"Wait?" She pulled my arm, tugging like she'd never let go. "What was that noise? Did you hear it?"

"No, I can only hear us breathing."

"It's across the hall, in that room." She pointed, and we crept to the door.

I turned the knob and swung the door wide. "Anyone in here?"

Harper hid behind me. "You go first. You're the brave one."

"Why does everyone keep saying I'm brave? I'm not."

"You are. I promise."

Then a soft sniffle made me hold my breath and bite my tongue. In the corner sat Jack, his eyes wide with fear and relief, and he motioned with a weak wave. "Help me. Someone hit me on the head, and I'm bleeding. I can't put any weight on my ankle, either." He pointed to his leg.

I knelt. "Jack! Who would have hit you?"

Harper echoed my question. "Who did this?"

"I don't know. Is that you, Harper?" Jack asked.

"Hey, Jack. I'm here for Christmas break."

Jack rubbed his head. "After I left down the alley, I realized I'd dropped my phone. When I returned, a boy with black hair stood at a window looking at me. I came inside, calling to him, but when I reached the top of the stairs, he tackled me. We wrestled, and that's the last I remember until a few minutes ago."

"You have a pretty deep cut on your head. You need a doctor."

Harper whined, "I hate blood. I pass out if I see blood. I can't do blood. Oh, gosh, blood … there's blood everywhere."

Jack whispered, "Harper. Seriously, will you ever toughen up?"

"No, I don't do tough. I came here for fun and Christmas; now we have blood."

I turned to Harper. "Stop and gather yourself. It's fine." I took a nearby dirty rag and pressed it on Jack's head. "Keep this over the cut. We should contact your dad. Did you ever find your phone?"

"No. I never found it."

I gazed at Harper. "Take a deep breath. Tell your grandparents that we need an ambulance for Jack and tell them to call the police about that boy."

"I can't move. I'm standing in a pool of blood."

I took her by the shoulders. "Focus. Try to stay with me. You're standing in a few drops of blood. You're fine. It's Jack who is bleeding. So, go get help." With that, I shoved the taffy into her palm. "Here, chew this and breathe."

Harper's braided hair waved as if she might faint, and she wiped her forehead. "I'll be right back. I'll get my grandma to call for help."

With Custard following me, I balanced Jack on one side, and we tried to hop, but Jack was taller than me, like everyone else, so I stopped and waited—the urgency of finding the lost boy who sprinted off to the woods no longer a priority. Saving Jack mattered most for now.

**

Later, as I stepped from the front porch at the Mitchell house, watching the fading, still flashing lights, I sighed as the ambulance, two fire trucks, and police car drove away. And somehow, I knew the banishment of going inside the Mitchell house was coming my way.

But I couldn't help but feel that this was just the beginning. With its creaking floors and secrets, the Mitchell house was more than just an old, abandoned house for sale. It was a mystery waiting to be solved, and Harper and I were at the heart of it.

"Harper, I know what we're doing on Christmas break. We're going to find the lost boy." I said, my determination fueling my words.

Harper nodded, her expression serious. "We're in this together, Emma. Whatever it takes, we'll find him. But I'm not sure he's nice. He hit Jack, remember?"

"True, but remember, that boy's gone through a horrible experience. Jack probably scared him." I countered, hoping I knew what I was saying.

With that, Mom waved for me to join her in walking home, and the questions about the boy who ran from its shadows pounded my every thought.

This wasn't the end. It was only the start of a Christmas we'd never forget. Custard nudged my leg, his ears on alert and his eyes on something in the woods.

Jack

TANGLED TRUTHS

I said goodbye to Harper and walked down Maple, ready to head home. Sensing the urgency, Custard pulled his leash taut as if he'd run off, given the chance. We were almost to my yard when two familiar figures appeared at the end of the street—Dylan and Duke, the notorious twins known for their knack of tying everything into knots, both literally and figuratively. The twins said that being in eighth grade does that to you when you're still treated like a kid, but feel you're nearly a teenager.

"Hey, Emma! What's the rush? You started an entire parade of fire trucks and ambulances earlier. What's up?" Dylan called out, a mischievous glint in his eye.

"Jack got hurt. He'll need stitches in his head, and his ankle will most likely receive a cast. But Harper and I saved him." My answer was smug, which Mom noticed, and she scolded me. "Emma, that tone needs to go."

Duke added, striding closer. "What's he got himself into this time?" Duke danced around me. "And Harper's in town?"

"Yes, for the holiday." I hesitated, unsure how much to share about our Tuesday morning plans, which she and I made before we parted for the night.

Known for their pranks, the twins were also surprisingly resourceful when they wanted to be. I exploded with the scoop, unable to keep my mouth shut. "We're going to search for that lost boy tomorrow. Want to help us?"

Dylan smiled. "The one from the poster?" He swallowed hard. "So, he is alive?"

"Yes, I saw him today. And he's out in the woods by the interstate by the Mitchell house."

Mom pulled on my arm. "Emma, the police will handle that search. You're not to go near those woods."

"But he was at the Mitchell house," I said, the words tumbling out in a rush. "He saw me. And I saw him. Maybe I can help."

The twins exchanged a look, their usual playful demeanor shifting to something more serious. Duke said, "The lost kid is Mark McIntosh. I saw it on the poster. I thought he was dead." When Duke said the word *dead*, his voice dropped an octave.

I sighed with a moan, thinking about how Mark must have watched his parents suffer. "Yes, we need to find him. He had a scared expression when he ran by me, resembling a person lost at sea." My throat quivered with worry, and I grabbed my neck.

The twins were momentarily silent, and then Duke said, "We'll help. We know the woods better than anyone. We used to play there before it got all creepy."

Mom reminded me and the twins. "I'm right here, walking with you three. Duke and Dylan, don't make me call your father. And Emma, tell me you'll drop this. Let the police do their job."

The twins said, "Yes, ma'am." I nodded and gave the twins my left-eye wink, which meant check your Facebook messenger when you get home.

With a new sense of purpose, I waved goodbye to the twins, and at home, I explained the situation to Dad. "I only went to find Jack, which I did, but now Mark needs my help."

Dad hit mute on the remote. "Seriously, leave this to the police. They'll find the boy and return him to his family."

I argued, "What if he has no one else? What if he's an orphan now?"

"Emma, your part in this might be to pray for Jack and Mark. And maybe you need to call it a night and get a good night's sleep. You've had an exhausting and busy day."

I trooped to my room, remembering that Harper and I made plans to set out again after breakfast. I sent the twins a text on Messenger on my iPad, along with Sebastian, and added Harper in the mix to ensure we'd meet at sunrise. The team of Lick Skillet investigators would head back to the Mitchell house—to scour the woods and collect clues.

I sighed and plopped back on my bed, wishing for a cell phone of my own. I could contact my friends so much faster if I had one.

The sun was gone, and Mom called from the living room. "You have fifteen minutes. Brush your teeth and let Custard out for his last potty break." Mom's words rattled; her shaky tone rippled with a firmness.

"Yes, ma'am."

I stood on the back patio, the shadow of the trees stretching across the sky like dark fingers, ready to grab me. My house was safe, but not far away in the short distance on Maple Street, a two-story house with dark windows and plenty of secrets called to me. It's as if my name rippled in the breeze.

From across the fence, a voice startled me. "Emma, I just heard that Jack got injured today." Jane clutched her guitar as if she might play a song, but she strummed three notes and sighed.

I stumbled, catching myself. "Yes, ma'am. He's going to be fine." I spoke to Jane, the neighbor I knew absolutely nothing about—except that she was in a photograph with Joyce Mitchell, and I knew she watered her flowers in spring and kept her curtains drawn—who played a song with sad notes and short, quick strokes on the strings of her guitar way too often.

Whenever Jane needed insight or confirmation about gossip, she talked to me from across the chain-link fence, her blonde hair mixed with some gray, like teeny wires of old age, slipping in, wild and unkempt.

Jane chimed in, the words escaping from her mouth, ready to check what I knew—to help fill in the blanks. "I've also heard the boy from the wreck is alive. Did you see him? I heard he's been hiding in the Mitchell house. I hope he's not hurt. I guess everyone thought he'd died in the wreck." She wiped her eyes and didn't wait for me to answer. She asked, "Did he seem—?" Jane's words trailed off like a series of lost musical notes.

I ran my hand through my hair. "How did you find out so fast that I saw the lost boy?"

"It's a small town. Lick Skillet has lots of talkers."

I wiped my brow, answering her as if I should. "The boy's eyes were wide, and his arms were swinging, then he ran off. He doesn't know us, so he's probably afraid."

"I sure hope he's okay. I'm worried ... and I've prayed for him since I heard about the wreck." She placed her hand over her heart and sighed.

"Yes, ma'am. The police are searching the woods for him tonight." I added my small talk, and Custard did his business in the yard. "Night, Jane."

"Good night." She held her guitar, her wrinkles like small canyons on her face—her smile nice. "Let me know if you learn what happens to the boy. I hate that he's going through this right now. Poor thing. If I can help, let me know."

"I will. I'm sure the newspaper will write a story. The reporters were there right after the ambulance came for Jack."

"You and your friends … know things before others catch wind. Let me know the latest. If you will."

"Okay," I coaxed Custard inside and back into my room, and on my iPad, I typed to the group: Don't forget. If the police don't find Mark by morning, meet me at the end of Maple. Dylan, Duke, and Harper gave me a thumbs-up emoji, but Sebastian never did. Mom called, "Lights out, Emma. It's time for bed."

**

After breakfast, I placed the leash around Custard, ready to rush to Maple Street. "I'm taking Custard for a walk," I told Mom, knowing part of my outing included a walk with my dog—and more. At the edge of the woods, my team of friends waited for me, and I rushed to meet up with them.

Wearing a bright yellow sweatshirt and jeans, Harper threw up her hands. "You're late. You're always late."

"I couldn't get out of the house. Mom had me put dishes in the dishwasher and she had me make my bed. Who makes their bed on Christmas break?"

Duke suggested, "We'll split up. Dylan and Harper, you two check the woods. Emma, you and Custard, come with me. We'll take the house."

I scratched my head. "I guess Sebastian went to the library. I thought he'd join us. But oh, well."

Splitting up felt risky, but it made sense. We needed to cover more ground quickly. With a nod, we parted ways, Harper and Dylan disappearing into the thickening trees, although with the yellow hoodie, Harper stood out like a target. Duke, Custard, and I approached the front porch of the Mitchell house—where a police officer stood—ready to shun us away. "We've searched for the boy. Are you the kids who saw him?" The officer asked.

"We didn't see him. Not properly. He ran by us. But Jack Cleverton saw him, up close, until he blacked out."

Custard growled when the officer petted his head. "Nice doggie. You don't bite, do you?"

I pulled on the leash. "Well, Custard has bitten anyone, yet."

Duke motioned for me to follow him. "Let's go, Emma. Let the officer do his job."

The man with the badge said, "There's no sign of the lost boy. Maybe your little friend, Jack, saw a ghost." The officer grinned as if he didn't believe the report from last night.

"Jack saw him. That's for sure." I argued while Custard sniffed the ground around my feet.

The officer pounded from the porch. "We've called off the search. There's no sign of the boy. I'm the last to leave."

I sucked in the wintry morning air, and the useless words I wanted to spew remained trapped inside my mouth—no need to give the officer a reason to stay by saying ugly things to him.

The patrol car drove away, and we moved to the backyard, the Mitchell house to ourselves—and I pushed the back door open—the flashlight ours to use. "Duke, this flashlight has me wondering. Do you think someone put fresh batteries in this? If it's been sitting here for months and years, the flashlight wouldn't work. The batteries would be dead."

"Maybe Mark found some. Or got some. Or had some. You overthink." Duke walked ahead, snatching the flashlight. "So, where did you find Jack yesterday?"

"This way." I hurried to keep up with Duke, his red hair appearing orange behind the flashlight's glow. "Jack was upstairs in that room."

The air inside was stale, filled with the scent of old wood and all those forgotten memories. We moved cautiously, our footsteps echoing in the quiet. "If I were a scared kid, I'd hide somewhere small, somewhere I felt safe," Duke muttered.

We checked closets, under beds, behind curtains, and anywhere a frightened person might seek refuge. But the house was silent, except for the creaks and groans from where we stepped. I whispered, "I don't think he came back here unless he snuck in last night after everyone went home."

"How old is this boy, anyway?" Duke asked. "I've forgotten."

"He's twelve but seemed younger, like eight or nine. Maybe they got that part wrong."

"Or maybe he's short like you."

"Or maybe you're wrong." I barked, and Custard growled at Duke as if he understood my annoyance.

Custard suddenly stopped, and his ears perked up. He sniffed the air, then let out a soft whine, tugging at his leash towards a closed door by a window.

"Duke, look," I whispered, pointing to Custard. Duke nodded, and we slowly approached the door, my heart pounding.

I reached out, my hand trembling, and pushed the door open. The room was dark, the curtains drawn, but a tiny figure huddled in the corner.

Inching slowly toward the shadow, I stopped. "It's okay. We won't hurt you," I whispered as Duke watched intently by the door.

The boy looked up and squinted, his gaze locked on me. It was him, the boy from the poster. His clothes were dirty and torn, and he looked like he hadn't eaten in days.

"My name's Emma, and this is Duke, and my dog, Custard. We want to help you," I said, keeping my voice soft.

Mark didn't speak; he stared at us, his body tensing like a deer ready to bolt. I knelt, trying to make myself as non-threatening as possible. "Can you tell us your name?"

After a long pause, he said, "Mark."

Relief washed over me. "Mark, we've been looking for you. Everyone thought you were ... that you didn't make it. But you're here. You're alive."

Mark's eyes filled with tears, and he nodded slowly. "I didn't know where to go. After the accident, I just ran. I was so scared."

Duke stepped forward, his expression softening. "It's okay, Mark. We'll get you some help, get you back to your family."

But Mark shook his head fiercely. "No! They're gone. All gone. I saw the fire. My parents were in the car. I got tossed to the ground. Flames were everywhere. I can't go back to ... to nothing."

My heart ached for him. He'd been through so much. "You're not alone, Mark. We're here, and we'll figure this out together," I promised, reaching out my hand.

He hesitated, then slowly, cautiously, placed his trembling hand in mine, and with Duke's help, we led Mark out of the room and down the stairs.

Outside, the sky had turned a deep blue, and the sun warmed up the cold air like spring had come early. Harper and Dylan emerged from the woods, and when they saw Mark, their eyes widened in shock.

"We found him," Duke said, with a note of triumph.

We all gathered around Mark, forming a protective circle. He looked at each of us, his eyes still filled with tears. And he shook like Custard did when I first found him. I reached for the taffy in my pocket. "Here, eat these. I bet you're starving."

Mark crammed the pieces of candy into his mouth faster than he could unwrap them. "Cinnamon! I didn't know I liked cinnamon this much."

"We need to call the police and let them know Mark's safe," I said, turning to Harper and the twins since they had cell phones.

Mark pulled a phone from his jeans pocket. "I found this in the yard. The battery's dead now, but I think it belongs to the boy who attacked me."

I spun like a top. "My friend Jack said you tackled him." I took the phone and put it in my pocket.

"Well, we collided, but I didn't know who he was, and he was yelling, and I didn't know what to do. He fell and hit his head on a dresser."

I countered, "Jack said you hit him in the head."

"No, I didn't. I promise. When Jack fell and didn't move, I thought he was dead, so I hid until I heard you calling for him. Then I ran. Everywhere I go, bad things keep happening."

Duke dialed his cell phone, and Mark tugged at my sleeve. "Please, tell me. Will I go to jail?"

I touched his shoulder. "You won't go to jail. Jack's ankle will heal, and his head will be fine. It was an accident."

Tears welled up in my eyes as I looked at his pleading face. What were we going to do? We couldn't keep Mark hidden away, but I couldn't bear the thought of sending him to another place where he'd be alone.

Duke's phone lit up, and then the caller on the speaker at the police station answered, "What's your emergency?"

I sighed with a gasp. "Hang up. Hang up."

Duke apologized to the voice on the other end. "I'm sorry. I dialed the wrong number." Duke pressed the end call button and turned to me. "What should we do?"

I hesitated, unsure of what to say. But then I decided. "Mark, you were lost and alone, but now you're safe. I'm taking you to my house. Let's see how my mom and dad can help make this better."

Harper pulled out a hand full of taffy. "Hey, here's some more taffy. Emma keeps all of us with cinnamon taffy. It's the best."

Mark unwrapped five more pieces without saying a word.

"We'll stay with you, Mark. You won't be alone," Harper said, squeezing his hand. "We'll walk with you to Emma's house."

As we made our way to my street, we met Mom at the door, whose eyes grew more prominent than a laundry room full of suds. She ushered Mark inside, where he stood sandwiched between us, and I knew our adventure was far from over.

We'd uncovered one mystery, but so many questions remained unanswered. Where will Mark go? What will his life look like from now on? I had many questions, but most likely, Mark had more than any of us.

I felt a stronger sense of purpose as I watched Mark chew and smack on a second peanut butter and banana sandwich and down his third glass of milk.

Eventually, Duke and Dylan went home, and Harper did, too, while Custard ate breadcrumbs beneath the table from the pieces of bread that crumbled through Mark's fingers as he shoved the food into his mouth.

Mark McIntosh was no longer a shadow, whisper, or face on a poster. He was real; he was here, and he was ours to protect. Somehow, I needed to convince Mom and Dad that Mark should have my baby brother's old room and stay here. But that was a long shot, at least for now.

As I considered the smudges of ash on Mark's face, I remembered that Sebastian never showed up. "Hey, Mom. Did Sebastian call you? Or come by?"

"Yes, you were supposed to go to the library for tutoring again. Remember? And now, you've missed studying for the second time." Mom hugged me from the side. "But it seems this rescue was a far better idea than doing math or history. Thankfully, it worked out like it did—especially for Mark."

With food in his mouth, Mark chomped, "This is the best peanut butter ever!" But then, he paused mid-chew and cried as if he'd never empty all his tears or be the same again.

Jane Hendershot

ECHOES OF THE PAST

Tonight, after several hours at the hospital where Mark got checked out, he received a clean bill of health despite some dehydration and a few cuts. And someone with authority let Dad bring him back to our house—for now.

Duke, Dylan, Harper, and Sebastian—one by one, returned to check on Mark too, and Mr. Cleverton stopped by for Jack's phone.

"Jack's ankle is broken," Mr. Cleverton said. "It's a hairline fracture; he'll wear a boot for six weeks."

Duke leaned close to me. "Mr. Cleverton doesn't want his little track star to miss out on any track meets."

"Duke, seriously. Be nice."

Dylan's shoulders shook. "That is nice for my brother."

"Dylan, you know that's true. Jack's dad wants him to be the best of the best." Duke wrinkled his nose and pushed

Dylan, adding one more remark, "Jack only runs those races to make his dad pay attention to him."

I shushed them. "Stop it. Both of you."

Mr. Cleverton moved to the front door, reaching for the handle. "Jack has fifteen stitches, too, but his hair will cover the scar. Thankfully, he is going to be fine." Mr. Cleverton glanced over and smiled at Mark. "You're not in any trouble. Boys will be boys. We're happy you're safe, too."

After Mr. Cleverton left, I whispered to Harper, the twins, and Sebastian, "We must ensure Mark stays safe. He must stay here. We have an extra bedroom."

Harper, her face etched with concern, echoed my worry. "He can't end up with some cold, unloving family."

Sebastian tapped my shoulder. "Emma, it's not our decision about what happens to Mark. When my grandfather disappeared last summer, I didn't have a say and ended up at my aunt and uncle's house."

"Yeah, but you love them. And they're family." I fidgeted, my hands itching to act. "Mark deserves a family."

Duke pulled on my ear as if he thought that would change my mind. "Emma. You are eleven. You don't have a say."

"I have a say because I have a voice. If I say nothing, then nothing can change. I will not be quiet."

Harper took both my hands. "Remember how I acted with all the blood around Jack? Now, you must breathe, calm down, and take your own advice."

Dylan nudged his brother. "Girls can be such a bother."

I countered, "And boys don't come with hearts."

Dylan put his hand to his chest. "I have a heart. But this is not something we get to decide—Mark's future is not in our hands."

A sudden knock interrupted our conversation, and Mom opened the door to find two police officers standing there, their solemn faces softening as they observed the scene inside.

Mom invited them in, and they introduced themselves to Mark, asking him more probing questions about the crash, his escape, and where he hid, which made me wonder how many times he would answer the same questions. This round of interrogation made Mark cry again, and his face turned red, so the officers stopped pressing him.

Mark had recounted his harrowing tale of fear, loss, and survival, and Custard nuzzled closer to him, sitting by his feet.

It was a slight gesture but spoke volumes about the bond—they both lost their family.

I moved and positioned myself next to Mark, who had a charm in the shape of a dog print hanging from a chain around his neck. "Do you have a dog?" I asked, the realization hitting me like a wave.

Mark looked up, his eyes meeting mine. "I had one. He was in the car …" His words trailed off, his tears falling like a waterfall, flooding the front of his shirt, and he choked on his words. "He must have … must have gotten trapped with my parents."

I handed him a paper towel to wipe his face. "I'm so sorry. So, sorry." I choked, crying with Mark. "Hey, Custard likes you. I'm sure he'd like to sleep with you tonight." My heart pounded like a car engine revving up inside my chest, one that might explode with flames. "Oh, Mark, I hate you are going through this."

Our conversation sent a ripple through the room, and a hush took over. But the connection between Mark and Custard wasn't just a coincidence. It was a thread linking them—a lost dog and boy needed each other on this gray night in December.

"So, what was your dog's name?" I asked, wishing I hadn't, wishing I could be quiet for once. But my words sprung faster than I could catch them, and my dad gave me the Hobbit glare, shaking his head.

In a low voice, Mark said, "His name was Goose."

"No way, Goose?"

"Yes, I first saw him chasing a goose two years ago. He never caught the goose, but I caught my dog. And the name stuck. He was yellow, with white paws and black patches on his ears." Mark rubbed Custard's ears—his snout appeared to smile when he gazed up at Mark. "Custard is a great name, too."

Having listened to Mark's story, the officers exchanged glances, each caught in the silence of their heartbeats—or was that mine? Mr. Officer said, "I'm sorry, but we must take Mark. There's been a change. He's staying with a foster family."

Mom interrupted, her voice firm yet compassionate. "Can't he stay here for the night? We were told he could stay. And besides, it's late, and the boy's been through so much. We have a spare room, and he seems to be comfortable here, and

Lord knows, he could use a good night's sleep," she said, pleading.

The officer made a call on his cell, muttering, then agreeing with someone, and turned to the room after ending his call. "Mark can stay for the night. We'll return in the morning to discuss further steps," the officer said, and the night filled offered a glimpse of hope again.

The magnitude of the situation sank in. Mark, a boy lost to the world, was sleeping under our roof, his past a broken puzzle, and his future missing certain pieces. And at the heart of it all was the old Mitchell house, a riddle of sadness that brought us together. Or so it seemed.

As Mom dashed across the room, she wrapped Mark in a tight bear hug while I redirected my focus to my friends. "We need to go back to the Mitchell house," I said, with determination. "There's something about that house that connects everything—that connects Mark and the accident. And we need to find out what it is. Even Custard keeps going there."

Harper and the twins nodded, their faces set with resolve. "We're with you, Emma. Whatever it takes," Dylan said, echoing the group's sentiment. Sebastian reminded me, "Tutoring. You have tutoring tomorrow."

I ignored Sebastian, and we made plans to revisit the Mitchell house, to peel back its layers of mystery and to see why Custard and Mark, or even me, felt the need to search there—especially since Mark told me earlier when I refilled his glass with milk, "We were on our way to see Joyce and Melvin because my mom and dad wanted me to know more about them. But then, the ... well, the wreck happened."

I scratched my ears, rubbed my eyes, and tucked away that part of the puzzle piece. I mean, who goes to see dead people?

**

The late December night turned colder, and now, I cried alone on the back porch, with only Custard noticing before he chased a bug in the yard. Letting others see me like this isn't a good idea for a lead investigator. I've got to be stronger than I feel, or I'll cry forever.

Looking up to heaven, I brushed my hair from my face. "Brett, your stuffed elephant is being safely kept on a shelf, which should make you happy. But I have some news. We have company. You would like him. But the boy is super sad. His parents are probably in heaven with you. His name is Mark. Tell his mom and dad that he is safe."

While I waited for Custard to explore the yard, I couldn't help but wonder how Mark escaped from the car the night his parents died. I took a deep breath. "Come on, boy. Let's go inside."

I stopped for a second, and through the dining-room window, its oversized panes allowed me to watch as Mark sat at our kitchen table eating a homemade chocolate chip cookie, his eyes red and cheeks flushed. He must have been taking in the scent of his new life—without his mom and dad. My heart was in my throat, and the thought of losing mine—too much to dwell on or consider.

Jane's porch light came on, and before I could get inside my house, she stepped outside, moving toward the chain-link. "I've heard that you found Mark. That he's not hurt. I've heard that Jack got hurt, though, and may have broken a bone in his foot, and he's received a head full of stitches, but he's going to live. But tell me, what's happening with Mark?"

I sighed, knowing that Jane only needed me to confirm her information. Sometimes, I think she's hidden a camera in my house since Jane has details about Lick Skillet almost before I do, but I know that's impossible.

"Hi, Jane. You're right. Mark was hiding at the Mitchell house, staying with us tonight. I'm not sure what's next. But he's safe. He's sleeping in my brother's room." Custard charged to the back door, his paws dancing with the goodnight-sleepy-time dance. "Well, I've got to go. See you later, Jane."

"Good night. Tell Mark I'm praying for him."

"I will."

As we sat in the living room, Mark fell asleep on the sofa in no time, with Custard by his side, a silent guardian in the night. Mom didn't insist on Mark brushing his teeth, which I never get away with—but I expect Mark would rest for the first time since the wreck. Maybe not entirely, but a little sleep would help. Mom yawned herself, and Dad helped Mark to bed in the room across from mine.

Later, I lay in my bed, the moon casting a pale glow through my window, and my thoughts raced like shooting stars. While Custard slept with Mark, I clutched my pillow, knowing that the Mitchell house was now connected to my life. So, I had to dig deeper. I felt a deep, unshakeable conviction that destiny was to bring some secrets to light. But would they help or hinder Mark's future?

**

The following day felt bright and clear, a stark contrast to the tangle of shadowy emotions within me. Harper and the twins gathered in the kitchen with me, a quick breakfast of Pop-Tarts and oatmeal punctuated by our shared determination. Mark, who appeared more rested, came to the kitchen. "Did I miss breakfast?"

I pushed Duke from his chair. "No, sit here. You're just in time."

Duke pulled a chair back from the other end of the table, giving me the twin glare, but held his sharp tongue and said nothing ugly to me—probably because Mark was with us.

Mom spooned oatmeal into a bowl for Mark. "This will warm you. Do you like sugar in your oatmeal?"

"Yes, please. And some milk."

I continued our planning in the living room, away from Mark's ears. "We'll divide into two groups," I said, laying out the scope of our next investigating phase. "Harper, you and I will take the inside of the house this time. Dylan and Duke, you guys cover the grounds. See if we missed anything."

Mom's hand landed on my shoulder. "Didn't we have this little chat? You're not about to get in the way over there? Or go back to the Mitchell house? Remember, before your dad left for work, he gave you those instructions."

"But we're just checking things out. We won't get in the way."

Mom grunted, moving to the kitchen to put the pan of oatmeal down, and smiled at me through the doorway. "Emma, I know it's hard for you to leave well enough alone. Just tell me you'll be careful."

I grinned. "I'll be careful. I promise."

Then Mark and Mom spoke of the hope of Mark staying longer, but none of us knew if that might happen, and in a few minutes, my friends and I barreled out the front door. "We'll be back in a while."

As we headed outside, Sebastian stood in the front yard with his backpack, and when he saw me, he yelled, "I knew it! I knew you'd miss day three of tutoring. So, I might as well go with all of you."

"Good, we could use your help."

We rushed to Maple Street, as Mom and Mark loaded up in the SUV to take care of paperwork at the police station.

Sebastian pulled on my arm as we rounded the corner. "Seriously, you must do some math and history before we go back to school. I want you to pass. Please tell me you'll try."

I smiled. "I'll try. But this is pressing."

As the five of us approached the Mitchell house, the two-story empty-for-sale home seemed to loom more prominent, more foreboding than before. With the peeling paint and cracked glass, the windows watched us like eyes full of deep secrets.

Harper and I entered first, the familiar scent of dust and old memories greeting us. We moved through the rooms with renewed purpose, examining every nook and cranny, searching for anything that might illuminate the mysteries.

Meanwhile, Dylan, Duke, and Sebastian scoured the grounds, searching. With its overgrown bushes and gnarled trees, the untamed garden seemed to ask more questions than it gave answers.

As Harper and I climbed the creaking staircase to the second floor, anticipation filled the air. Each step seemed to echo with a moan, and I wondered if the past, with the laughter and tears of those who'd once called this place home—left clues to help us know more. After all, Mark's family was coming here. Why would they do that?

We reached the room where we'd found Mark, the sunlight filtering through the dirty curtains and casting long shadows across the floor. I could almost feel Mark, who'd hidden here, his fear a tangible mist in the stale air.

"We're going to find answers," I whispered, more to myself than anyone. "We're going to make this right."

Harper questioned me. "I'm with you all the way. But I don't get what you think is happening here. Mark's parents died in a car crash, and Custard wandered off. It's just an old house—nothing to see or find."

"I sense it. There's a reason Mark's family planned to visit the Mitchells. I must know more."

Harper grabbed me. "Wait, how do you know that? Did Mark tell you his parents were coming here?"

"Yes, he let it slip out last night."

Harper cracked her knuckles and then shook me by the shoulders as if she'd rattle more secrets from me. "And you didn't tell me. Why wouldn't you?"

"I guess I forgot." I sighed, knowing I hadn't forgotten but could delay telling others certain things as I get protective of my clues.

"That's important. You should have told me."

"You're right. I should have told you. So much has happened, and so fast. Let's tell the twins and Sebastian. I shouldn't keep secrets if we're going to help Mark unravel the secrets and how he's connected to Lick Skillet."

Emma, Jack, Sebastian, & Harper

WHO'S KEEPING SECRETS NOW

Downstairs, the sound of Dylan calling from outside stopped us just as we reached the top of the staircase. "Emma! Harper! You need to see this!"

We hurried out to the backyard and found the twins and Sebastian standing by the decrepit shed next to the trees at the edge of the property. "Look," Duke said, pointing to the ground.

A small, weathered metal box peeked at us from the dirt, half-buried under a pile of leaves, and Sebastian folded his arms. "Someone hid this box."

I countered his comment. It may have fallen off a shelf in the shed and got buried under debris from the past few storms.

Dylan held the box, and Duke opened the lid, and Harper reached for the papers. "These papers are wet, but look, there are photographs."

As we sifted through the contents, a picture caught my eye. It was a family portrait, the faces hauntingly familiar. A couple with a baby, their smiles wide and carefree. Who were they?

"Harper, look at this. It's got to be a picture of Mark. He's just younger. And Joyce and Melvin are sitting on the swing with him on the front porch of this house!"

Sebastian gulped hard. "I don't remember my parents that much, but I have pieces of memories. Mark may remember this day."

Harper outstretched her arms and hugged Sebastian. "Gosh, this must feel weird for you, too. Emma told me about your grandpa and his memory loss and how your parents died when you were younger."

Sebastian sighed. "Emma's not much for keeping a secret. But she is the reason my grandpa is safe now. I must give her that."

I jumped up and down. "That's it. This is a memory for Mark. He'll want this box with the letters and photos." Then I gulped super hard, my neck stretching with the ache of knowing I had a piece of truth I'd not shared. "Umm, guys,

Mark told me he and his parents were going to see the Mitchells when the car crash happened."

Duke rebuked me, waving his arms. "No way. The Mitchells are dead."

Dylan danced in a circle around me. "You're making that up. Why are you saying such a thing?"

"I'm not making it up. Mark told me last night. I don't think he knew, or his parents did, that the Mitchells were gone."

Sebastian took the photograph from my hand. "So, Mark has visited the Mitchell house before? What else is he not telling us?"

Duke chimed in. "He's on the run. Mark's a thief. He's hiding something. He's got to be up to no good." Dylan added, "That's right. Why wouldn't he say something?"

I piped in. "I just told you. Mark told me they were on their way to the Mitchell house. But that's all he said."

Harper brought a voice of reason. "Duke, stop judging Mark. He doesn't owe us anything. We've accused him of attacking Jack, and his parents are dead. He's not obligated to share his past just because we found him. Let's cut him some slack."

I dug through more pictures, listening to my friends analyze Mark, and yes, standing beside Joyce and Melvin in another photo, once again, a person I recognized—it was Jane, like in the photograph on the staircase inside the house.

Many connections clicked into place, and each discovery added ten more questions to my thoughts. The Mitchell house had memories intertwined in unexpected, often tragic ways. I held my breath. "Hey, I wonder if Mark, his parents, and their dog, Goose, were coming here to buy this house? Maybe that was it?"

Harper shook her head. "But why? That doesn't seem likely since Mark didn't mention he might move here."

Duke agreed. "Yeah, that's it. They were buying this house."

Dylan slapped his brother on the back. "That's got to be it. They were moving here. They were the new owners."

Shaking my head, I countered. "Seriously, why don't we ask Mark instead of pretending we have the answer? We do not know what's happening or about to happen to Mark, for that matter."

We returned to my house with the box and the photos, a treasure of clues in our quest for understanding. Mark's eyes filled with tears as we laid the contents on the floor. "That's them," he said, his voice barely a whisper, "Joyce and Melvin."

We gathered around him, a circle of support, and yet, my mind raced with questions. "So, you knew Joyce and Melvin?" I placed my hand on his shoulder. "Just tell us how we can help."

"I know them, but not really." Mark sighed.

The day's endless questions included nods, tears, and a few answers. We skimmed over the papers and photographs, piecing together the story as Mark shared parts of his life.

A photograph linked Mark's past with the present, and the Mitchell house was more than just a place with whispered surprises and hidden truths. It was a crossroads, a point where paths diverged and converged in the most unexpected of ways.

As we sat there, surrounded by the echoes of the past, I knew our journey was far from over.

Mark bit his fingernails. "We haven't been here in years. I barely remember them. But the Mitchells are—were my grandparents, and we didn't know they had died or that the house was for sale. Mom and Dad wanted me to know them— so we packed up and made the trip from Oklahoma."

I cradled Custard and placed him across Mark's crossed legs. "Here, this puppy needs a hug."

"You're right," Mark said, his tears dropping like summer rain onto the coat of a dog who reached up with a paw to catch each tear.

Then, an engine roared, and a sharp sound of brakes squeaking told me a car had pulled up outside. I ran to the curtain—the blinds were open from earlier in the day, and one officer from the night before stepped out, his face stern and official.

He approached the door, and Mom ushered him into the living room where we all sat, the box's contents spread out before us. Mark's hands went through his black hair. Sensing his distress, Custard nudged Mark's hand, licking his fingers.

The officer said, sighing a little. "Good evening. I'm here to take Mark with me. We have a more permanent situation in place for him."

The room fell silent, the gravity of the officer's words crushing my ability to take a breath. I screamed, "No way! You can't take Mark from us. Will you please decide, once and for all—that he can stay with us?"

Mark looked down, his hands clenched tightly in his lap. The thought of his being taken away from the safety and warmth of my house, from us, terrified me.

"But he's safe here," I protested, my voice trembling with emotion. "Can't he just stay with us? At least until you find more family members?"

The officer exchanged a glance with Mark, his expression softening slightly. "I understand that you've formed a bond with Mark," the officer said. "But we have protocol to follow. It's for his safety."

Mom stepped forward, her demeanor calm but resolute. "Officer, my husband and I will be Mark's temporary guardian if you can make that happen. We can provide a safe place during his transition. Isn't that better than sending him away?"

The officer hesitated, clearly torn. The room was thick with tension, each of us holding our breath, waiting for the response. We now stood in a circle around our new friend.

Until now, Dad, who had slipped in from work about an hour ago, kept quiet, but thankfully, when he has something important to say, people listen. "The boy needs a place to feel safe. You'll know he's with us. Carl, you've known me for a long time. I'm not going anywhere with the boy. Why don't you call and see if we can work this out?"

I hugged my daddy around his waist, never so proud and happy he was mine. "Mark needs to stay with us," I added, my voice stern, not as nice as my dad's tone.

Carl responded, "I'll need to discuss this with my supervisor. I can't make any promises."

The officer stepped outside to make the call; the weight of the situation pressed down on us. Mark looked at me, his eyes meeting mine, a silent plea for reassurance. I whispered, "It's going to work out. We won't let them take you away. You belong here, with us."

As we waited, the minutes seemed to his pause, like time stopped, making my heart pound like a drum. Eventually, the officer came back, his expression impossible to figure out.

"I've spoken with my supervisor," Carl began. "Given the unique circumstances of this case, your permission to keep Mark is in place. Keep in mind, this is temporary."

A sigh of relief filled the room. Mark's shoulders raised, his chin too, and the tension draining from him lifted as he smiled. A sly glint in his eyes revealed a sparkle as he realized he could stay.

"However," Carl continued, "Don't forget, this is only temporary. We'll need to fully investigate who his relatives are and find a suitable long-term solution for Mark."

Mom nodded, her expression serious. "Understood. We'll cooperate in any way we can." Dad moved to Mom's side, and my parents became a statue of courage for Mark.

The officer left, and the room erupted into hoots, hollers, and high-fives between Mark and me.

Mark looked around at us, his eyes shining with unshed tears. "You fought for me," he said, turning to my parents, his voice barely above a whisper. "Why?"

"I believe we're in your life for a reason. And you're in ours. You belong to us, and in the future, you will still be part of our family," Dad said as he rustled Mark's hair, wiping a tear from his eye.

Harper bounced like a rabbit and said, "That's right, you're one of us now," her voice was firm and sure. "You're part of the Lick Skillet family."

As the night drew in, Harper and the twins went home, but Sebastian cornered me for a few minutes of algebra and Texas history. I responded after the quizzing, "Seriously, you're going to make an outstanding teacher one day, but I would hate to be in your class."

"At least you would learn and make better grades. That's important."

"I'm not really into math or history, but I love puzzles and solving mysteries."

Sebastian swung his backpack onto his shoulders. "Who knows? You might change your mind one day."

Laughing, I giggled with a burping sound. "I'm not so sure of that." That's when Mark added, "I love math and history. I love to read, too."

For a brief second, I wondered if math, history, and reading—could change my life. But only for a second did I even consider such a thought.

Sebastian took off for home, and Mom, Dad, and I gathered around Mark, a makeshift family united by circumstances and an old house.

As the Mitchell house and its mysteries still loomed in my mind, I wondered how Jane fit into the picture—but so far, Mark's given me only small parts of his life, but trust is growing.

Outside, I paced on the back porch again, as it seemed I often come to the backyard, probably because my alone time lets me hide in plain sight. I waited for Custard to take care of his business, too, and the stars twinkled in the night sky, a reminder of the world beyond my little town. But inside, hope filled the house, a beacon of light in the darkness.

And at one point tonight, I heard Mark whisper to Custard. "We'll find our way, Goose. I'll be long gone next time the officers come for me."

I should run inside and tell Mom and Dad what Mark said, but he's faced so much that being a tattle-tell won't help our friendship. I'll keep a close eye on him, though.

As I finally lay in bed, the day's events replaying in my mind, I realized there were still so many questions I wanted to ask, and I also wanted to interview Jane to see what she knew about Joyce and Melvin.

My eyes got heavy, and I yawned bigger than I had in days, but then I heard a creak across the hallway from my bedroom. I crept to the door, opening it, only to see Custard nestling next to Mark in the shadows.

Clothed in a fresh shirt, jeans, and tennis shoes, Mark stopped and put his finger to his lips to hush me.

I whispered, "Mark, what are you doing? And where are you going?"

"The police keep trying to take me away. I'm leaving before the officers return for me. And keep this to yourself. This is my life. Not yours. Please?"

Emma

INTO THE SHADOWS

I blocked the hallway in my orange and green checkered pajamas, and Mark froze in the dim light of a nightlight. He was carrying a backpack, an old one Sebastian had given to him. He held Custard's leash with his other hand and looked at me, his eyes filled with tears, and his hair waved from his wobbly stance. "Emma, I have to do this," he whispered. "I have to find out the truth—to who I am and where I fit in."

"You can do it in the daylight. It doesn't have to happen now. Besides, you saw the Mitchells and know there's more to your story, but sleep—you need a good night's sleep."

"But you don't know everything. It's my fault. All of it." Mark said as he sucked in a deep breath, so much so he coughed.

"Mark, you can't just leave," I protested, stepping closer to him. "My parents made sure you could stay, and now you leave. Why? I don't understand."

He shook his head, a stubborn set to his jaw. "You don't understand, Emma. The memories keep returning, those from inside the car before the accident. I argued with my parents, and I kept urging my father to stop the car—to tell me more about my past. I pressed him with too many questions, and he let go of the steering wheel with one hand, and then, the next thing I knew, the car skidded to the shoulder, and he lost control. Did you hear me? He lost control! What if it's all my fault? And if it is, they will send me away."

I reached out, trying to offer some comfort. "Mark, memories can be misleading, especially from a car accident. We can figure this out together. You're not alone."

He looked down, gripping Custard's leash. "I need answers, Emma. There are too many parts of my past that I don't understand. I think I know where to start. McIntosh isn't my real last name if you've read anything in the paper about my story. It's Mitchell. Everyone who reads the newspaper now knows I'm adopted—or that I was by Eddie and Sandra McIntosh, thanks to that one news reporter."

I blocked his way, holding my arm out. "Last names mean nothing—" I thought about what Mark said, unsure how I missed such an important detail from the newspaper story.

Mark pushed me aside. "—Or they mean everything. I overheard my parents talking around Thanksgiving, arguing about how old I'd be when they told me."

"When they told you what?"

"Emma—when they told me about my adoption," Mark said, his face red like catsup. "Joyce and Melvin are my biological grandparents. We visited occasionally a long time ago—not that I remember much. My birth mom was their daughter-in-law—and she's not in any of those photos. I don't have any idea who she is! I don't even know her name!"

Gulping, I wiped the sweat from my face, and his words slapped me like a wave of burning ash from a fire. "So, you think the Mitchell house has more answers about your adoption?"

He nodded slowly. "Yes. I need to understand why my adoptive parents kept it from me, why everything was such a secret. And I need to do this on my own."

"Are you coming back?" I wiggled in my socks. "You have my dog on a leash. You must come back. Besides, what would I tell my mom and dad?"

Mark moved forward, bumping my shoulder, and placed the leash in my hand without answering. He then rushed out the front door, disappearing down the street. "Wait, you can't go," I said, stepping onto the porch as Custard whined beside me.

I stared into the darkness, torn between following him and respecting Mark's need to face this alone. But the worry gnawed at my heart and became too intense to ignore. So, I grabbed my jacket, slipped on my shoes, and followed him into the night, wearing my PJs from last year with Custard bouncing along next to me as if this were his idea.

The streets were empty, bathed in the soft glow of the streetlights. Some houses left their Christmas lights on at night, which laced the sidewalks with different shades of color. I hurried purposefully, running towards the old Mitchell house.

Mark, just ahead of me, hesitated as he reached the property, then stepped across the yard. The house held a dark silhouette contrasting with the night sky. I followed quietly, my heart pounding with panic and willpower.

I waited momentarily until Mark slipped into the back door, and then I found Mark in the living room, the moonlight casting long shadows across the hardwood floor.

As if he talked to someone, Mark said, "I need to know why. Why they never told me, why everything had to be such a secret."

I stepped into the room, and my presence caused him to spin like a top. "Emma, what are you doing here?" he asked, his surprise clear by the high pitch in his voice.

"I couldn't let you do this alone," I said, moving closer. "Whatever you find, whatever happens, I'm here for you, Mark."

He looked at me with gratitude and concern in his eyes. "I don't want to drag you into this, Emma. It's my problem."

I shook my head, unwavering. "Friends share things. You don't have to do this alone."

"But we haven't been friends that long. You don't have to act like you care."

"I'm not acting. I wouldn't have come if I didn't want to be your friend. So, guess what? I'm not leaving."

We moved through the house together, the surrounding silence almost tangible. Each room we entered felt charged with the echoes of the past, the heaviness of untold stories pressing down on us. No Christmas lights. No Christmas tree.

No presents. And no candy canes. But we had the lone flashlight that showed us the way.

Mark broke the silence. "Let's go upstairs. I stayed here several days before you showed up—searching. But so far, I haven't found a thing that tells me who my mom is or why she gave me away."

"Let's look at every corner, then, for clues."

Finally, we reached what must have been Joyce and Melvin's bedroom. The air felt heavier there, the shadows deeper. Mark approached an old desk, the moonlight illuminating a stack of papers through the window.

"Have you looked through these?" I asked.

"Yes, but go ahead. I could have missed something." Mark picked the stack of papers up, his hands trembling slightly. "These are old letters and utility bills," he said, his voice catching.

We sat on the floor, flipping through papers, and I found a letter from Sandy to Joyce. "Look, your mom wrote this letter. It's her talking about your baseball games."

"Unreal! I didn't know they kept in contact like that."

The letter mentioned how Sandra and Eddie planned to tell Mark about his adoption before he got much older, confirming what Mark knew—that Joyce and Melvin were his biological grandparents. But who was his birth mother?

I stretched out on my stomach, leaning on my elbows, and my foot bumped a book beneath the desk's center. "What is this?" I reached into the dark spot in the corner. "It's a diary." I flipped through the pages, and a photo floated onto our stack of papers.

Mark grabbed it. "This is a baby with his mother."

I leaned in. "He has your black curls. Maybe it's you with your real mom?"

"Who knows?" Mark sighed, staring at the image as Custard licked his face.

The diary pages were lengthy and held the most profound revelations. It belonged to Joyce, and in the diary, she wrote of the pain of losing her son, Darien, to cancer before her grandson was born.

Then, the decision to have Mark adopted by a family they knew was on a page that told how Mark's birth mother disappeared—without a word. I turned to Mark after reading parts out loud to him. "Do you think your biological mom couldn't handle Darien's death? Maybe she went to a dark place during that time?"

"A dark place? How does a mother leave her baby?"

I swallowed hard, knowing I had nothing more to say to help make Mark feel better. I read on silently, yet that one photo showed me his birth mom had held Mark—but why would she go away?

The Mitchells kept Mark for ten months, and Eddie and Sandra McIntosh adopted Mark right before his first birthday. "Mark, your real mom's name isn't on any of the pages, and I can't find any notes in the diary after April 2020. That's about the time your grandparents caught the virus, and they both died during the summer. It's almost the year 2024 now, and your adoptive parents didn't know they'd died. How could that be?"

Mark held up that one photo. "I guess my parents just assumed the Mitchells were alive. We're not a close-knit family. Despite that, I have one photo of my birth mother— someone must know her." Mark yanked the diary from my hands. "Who is … my actual mother?"

I searched for helpful words. "When your real dad died, it's like she did too. We don't know what that did to her."

"She gave up. I was a baby. And she abandoned me."

"Maybe she wanted to come back. We don't know what happened to her. She left you with your grandparents, in their care, and they loved you and protected you."

As we read, flipping through pages again, out of order and in random segments, the first light of dawn edged across the sky, casting a soft, diffused streak of the morning into the room. Mark's face was a mix of emotions and understanding but also laced with sorrow. "I want to forgive my birth mom, but honestly, I'm struggling."

"I'm sorry this is happening, but you had years of love with your adoptive family. That's a glorious memory."

Mark sighed and swallowed hard. "Emma, my adoptive parents loved me. I know that's true." His voice trailed; his words barely audible above a whisper. "They loved me so much they kept the secret to protect me from the pain of knowing my actual mother didn't want me."

I reached out, squeezing his hand. "They loved you, Mark. Try to remember the good."

"But I can't help but wonder if my birth mother is alive and if I could ever find her." He clutched the diary, tucking it into his backpack. "Her name must be in here somewhere."

The morning light grew stronger, filling the room with a sense of new beginnings. We uncovered facts and truths that brought more pain, but this path might lead to a home for Mark.

We stepped outside, the morning sun warming our faces. We needed to return to my house before my mom and dad got up—before they knew Mark and I had been gone all night.

Custard tugged on the bottom of Mark's shirt as if to say don't leave—come home. After a short walk, we returned to my house with new secrets and a few answers—yawning from staying up all night.

THE LONG JOURNEY HOME

The morning sun streamed through my bedroom window as I lay there, as we'd barely returned to the house before Dad's alarm beeped. My thoughts swirled through my mind, and I hoped Mark had stayed put in the other bedroom.

I'm sure he's exhausted from the revelations of the night. I know I am, and part of me knew I'd tell my mom the entire story of sneaking off, too. Keeping secrets from her is never easy.

I moved to Mark's bedroom door, tapping, and didn't wait for an answer. I walked right in, studying his face. He appeared relaxed in sleep. Custard curled closer, snuggling at Mark's feet, not wanting to get up.

My heart ached for Mark and all he had endured. The secrets uncovered at the Mitchell house had only made Mark feel rejected, but who was his birth mother? Why had she disappeared from Mark's life? And what were we going to do now?

A soft woof broke the silence. I looked over to see Custard — lift his head. His brown eyes met mine, so full of warmth, and my mind reeled as I patted Custard's head. "Get some rest, buddy."

I fell asleep faster than I could take the next breath, but a soft tap across the hall on my bedroom door made me open my eyes, and Mom said, "Sleepyheads miss out on breakfast. It's nearly eleven."

I ached, not wanting to get up, and tried to stand. My socks were like skates on the hardwood floor. "Emma?" Mom's voice called, "Breakfast is ready. You and Mark, come and eat. You, too, have slept in."

A shallow tap across the hall told me Mom stood at Mark's door. "Come on, sleepyheads. It's a new day."

I hurried across the hall to wake Mark, shaking him gently. He sat up, disoriented, and jerked and whined like he was having a nightmare. "What are you doing, Emma?"

Whispering, I said, "I was just checking on you. We've slept all morning."

"I'm so tired. I could stay in bed all day."

I moved to the door. "We'll be right there," shouting to Mom as if everything in Lick Skillet were in order. "Hurry and get dressed, Mark—and about last night, we must tell my mom."

Mark wouldn't meet my eyes with his. "I just want my old life back."

My heart broke for him. "I understand why you had to go last night. But no more secret nighttime outings."

"All right. I'm so confused by all of this. It's horrible to think that no one is looking for me."

**

Over bowls of scrambled eggs, toast, and orange juice, Mark recounted an abridged version of last night's discoveries to my parents without my prompting, which kept me from explaining our secret mission to the Mitchell house.

They listened intently, their faces etched with compassion, but somehow, I knew Mom wasn't happy with me—her glances, squints, and pursed lips were a sign of a discussion she and I would have later.

"Mark, we want you to know that you have a home here as long as you need it," Dad said, his voice kind but firm. "We'll help you find out about your birth mother, too."

Mark ducked his head, blinking back tears. "You've all been so nice to me. I don't deserve it."

"Nonsense. You've been through things no child should have to endure. But you're safe here," Mom said.

Over the next few days, Mark got comfortable with us and completed interviews, appointments, counseling sessions, and a follow-up doctor's visit. My parents supported him, attending those meetings and ensuring Mark felt cared for and secure.

One afternoon, Mom entered the living room with a gentle smile. "Mark, I have great news. The police have located your birth certificate and adoption records. Your birth mother's name is Lydia Walsh. Does that sound familiar? She used her maiden name on your birth certificate. It had Walsh, not Mitchell."

Mark blinked hard; his face twisted into a confused look at Mom. "Know her? How could I? She left me with my grandparents, and she didn't want me. Why would I know her?" Mark folded his arms, frowning; his harsh response made my chest ache.

"Oh, sweetie," Mom said. "I'm so sorry. I didn't think this through. We'll take this one step at a time. That's a lot to take in." Mom gathered him in a hug, and, at first, Mark resisted, but then melted into her embrace.

True to their word, my parents cared for Mark, and yes, his temporary stay became longer and longer—with Christmas just ahead.

Harper and the twins visited often, bolstering Mark with friendship and companionship. And Custard practically glued himself to Mark's side, offering unconditional canine affection—but Custard also let me pet him as if to say—he loved me too.

Then, late one night, the doorbell rang. We opened it to find the same two police officers from earlier visits, their expressions friendly, yet I grew to dread their visits. Behind them stood a woman with strawberry blonde hair and a kind, weary face. "This is Lydia Walsh, Mark's biological mother," one officer said.

We stared in shock, and Lydia gave a sad smile. "I understand this must come as a surprise. Might I come in? There is much I need to explain."

As we sat tensely in the living room, Lydia began her story. She had fallen into a deep depression after Darien died. Convinced she could not care for a baby alone, she temporarily left him with her in-laws.

"I was grieving and felt so lost," she said, eyes downcast. "I planned to get back on my feet and return for you, Mark. But days slipped into months and years ..." She shook, retelling a story that made us all cry.

Custard jumped next to Mark at the end of the sofa, where Mark held him close. He asked in a low tone. "But you left me. Who does that to their son?"

"I wasn't in a good place. And once you got adopted, I didn't think I could ever be a part of your life."

Mark sobbed, and I sat next to him, plopping down between Lydia and Mark to protect him, wishing his pain would end.

She leaned forward and said, "I can't make amends for my years of absence. But I still hope ... I still wish ..."

Her words trailed off as Mark stood and slowly approached her. He extended his arms and hugged her, and Lydia broke into sobs, clutching her long-lost son—while Custard growled at Lydia's feet.

I pulled Custard away. "Stop that. It's okay, buddy."

Watching this reunion, I knew their road would be long and complicated, but Mark also had all of us by his side now.

Lydia said, "You look so much like your father."

As I listened to them talk, I secretly hoped she would truly move heaven and earth to help Mark heal.

Later that night, after Lydia had gone, Mark joined me on the back porch, and he sat down in a wrought-iron chair beside me, where Custard snuggled beside my feet. I felt the need to break the silence. "Quite a day, huh?"

Mark nodded. "I have a new mom, and I don't know how to react."

"She seems kind, plus she came searching for you the moment she could."

"It's weird though, I don't even know her." Mark inhaled and said, "Hey, Emma, thank you."

"For what?"

Mark smiled softly. "For finding me. For helping me uncover the truth. For being my friend." He chuckled like he was almost happy. "That first day I met you, I thought you were crazy, chasing Custard everywhere."

I laughed. "Well, life with Custard is always an adventure."

We then sat in contented silence for several minutes, and Mark turned to me, his expression growing serious. "Emma, I need to ask you something important."

I raised my eyebrows. "Sure, Mark, you know you can ask me anything."

He took a deep breath. "I hoped that maybe you'd let me keep visiting Custard. I know he's your dog, and I understand if you want me to back off. But he means a lot to me. He lost his family, and so did I. It might help me if we could hang out together." He bit his lip nervously. "So ... would that be, okay?"

Tears flooded my eyes, and I threw my arms around Mark's neck. "Of course, you can keep visiting Custard. He adores you."

Mark pulled away, almost as if the sorrow rose in him from every vein in his body, as if the idea of life without his parents might be too much to get over. So we both sat there on the porch as Jane played on her guitar in her backyard, and Custard let out tiny howls to sing along.

Although the old Mitchell House creaked in the distance, I felt a surge of gratitude. The mystery that started with a muddy dog led me to this extraordinary boy, who has quickly become a brother. We were now intertwined, our lives bound by a friendship forged through adversity.

However, I felt that Lydia Walsh had a secret. And I didn't know what to think—but something was wrong with their reunion. Even Custard growled at her—like he knew something didn't fit.

Besides, whenever my elbow itches, it's a sign that I must investigate further; right now, the itching is intense. So maybe it's time to talk to Jane and see what she knows about Lydia Walsh and if she could fill in the blanks about Mark's birth— to stop the constant itching on my arm.

Emma

AN UNEXPECTED VISIT

"Come on, guys, we have little time!" I shouted from the top of the stairs at the Mitchell house, where I had called the emergency meeting. Harper, Duke, Dylan, and Sebastian bounded up the stairs, and Jack clattered with his cast on his way to the second floor.

"Do we have to do this today?" Jack grumbled, adjusting the cumbersome boot cast. "Christmas is in two days. I've got presents to wrap."

Harper rolled her eyes. "Finding out about Mark's long-lost mother is more important than wrapping socks for your cousins, Jack."

I smothered a laugh.

Jack was no match for Harper's blunt answers, even though his sarcasm flies out faster than a track star can run when he's not injured.

"Emma's right, this is important," Dylan added. "Who knows when the thrift shop will be open again? It's right before the holidays, and this town shuts down for Christmas."

Sebastian asked, "Catch me up. What's with the thrift shop? And what are we doing?"

I pulled out taffy for each of them. "We know Lydia works there, so we're going shopping—to check her out. To follow her home. To see what she's made of—and if she's up to no good."

Dylan smacked on his candy as we sat in a circle cross-legged. "I bet she's a lifetime criminal." Duke gave Dylan a high-five and added, "Yes, a criminal. A mastermind. A thief. An alien."

Harper shook her head. "Duke, an alien?"

"She might be. Who knows?"

Earlier that morning, Harper asked her grandparents about the Mitchells and searched for details about Lydia. I turned to Harper. "So, what did you learn?"

"They know Lydia from church, not really well," Harper said. "She's quiet and keeps to herself. Lydia was gone for years and years but now works at the Corner Thrift Shop on

Front Street. Granny swears she saw Lydia at the grocery store last week with only milk and two cans of soup. She says Lydia struggles to pay her bills. And that she never says, y'all, but says you guys and has forgotten her roots."

I mouthed. "Sounds like we're gossiping and not investigating now."

Harper smiled. "I tell it like it is. Investigating means talking—any insignificant detail might be huge."

I added a new twist. "Everybody ready? Like Harper said, let's find out more about this Lydia Walsh."

Duke said, "Let's see if she might be an alien."

Dylan giggled like this would be the best fun, but it made me worry we'd cause more trouble than we should.

Mark went to church for a visit with my pastor, and my parents tagged along with him. So, it was the perfect chance to spy on Lydia.

After all, she'd abandoned Mark once before, even though she claimed to regret it. I had to know her intentions before she reentered Mark's world.

Duke suddenly snapped his fingers. "Guys, I have one of those tracking tags. We could put it somewhere in her car. And I could keep up with her on my phone."

We all stopped talking, giving Duke our confused looks, and he grinned mischievously. "What? We could slip a tracker in the car, and if she bolted again, we would know where she went."

"She showed up because the police found her. She's got regret." I said, hoping my words were true, but the tracking device sounded interesting.

Sebastian let out a breath of air like a whistle. "Let's just focus on finding out more about her first."

We reached the Corner Thrift Shop, an aged brick building jammed between a laundromat and a vacant building that used to be a craft store. Stepping inside, the stale air burned my nose, and rows of clothing, knick-knacks, and assorted junk greeted us.

"Keep your eyes peeled for employees," I said, and we fanned out, pretending to scrutinize the thrift store treasures. My friends' bizarre tastes soon had them oohing over odd items. Dylan became engrossed with a display of ties with

Looney Tunes characters on them. In his distraction, Jack, leaning on his cast, almost knocked over a tower of ceramic figurines. Duke made a beeline for the electronics section, probably seeking more tracking devices and other sneaky items. Harper kept eyeing the board games while Sebastian touched every book.

I was sorting through a cart of plush animals when a voice spoke behind me. "May I help you find anything?"

I whirled around to see a woman wearing a red vest with a name tag. It was Lydia. Lydia had her strawberry blonde hair tied in a ponytail and wore silver-rimmed glasses perched on her nose as if she were balancing the entire world. "Well, hi, it's Emma, right?"

"Uh, yes, ma'am. I'm finishing up my Christmas shopping."

"What are you looking for? We have some cute stuffed animals."

Mark's *new* mother seemed weary. Her eyes were ringed with faint dark circles, but her gaze was alert behind the glasses.

Realizing I was staring at her, I stammered, "Oh, no thanks, just browsing! I'm not sure what I'll buy." I hastily turned back toward the tiny stuffed animals, my mind racing.

What should I do? Call my friends over? Should I demand answers from Lydia about why she abandoned Mark? I'm a self-appointed investigator, but this might make Mark angry if he knew what I was doing. I don't have his permission to quiz Lydia.

As Lydia moved down another aisle, I made a snap decision and followed casually. Waiting until she had passed Duke, still engrossed in the electronics, I *accidentally* bumped into a display stand filled with greeting cards.

Lydia spun to the toppling stand, instinctively moving to help pick them up. As she knelt beside me, gathering cards, I decided on a more subtle approach.

"I can't believe it's already Christmas again," I babbled, playing up my accident-prone preteen image. "Seems like summer was just yesterday, you know? Time sure flies. Oh gosh, I didn't mean to interrupt your work! I'm so clumsy."

I studied Lydia's face from the corner of my eye, and she gave me a slight chuckle. "You're not clumsy. I spent many years in California and worked several jobs. Clumsy is my middle name." She coughed and cleared her throat. "So, would you like to buy a greeting card?"

I sucked in the dust from dropping all the cards. "Yes. I think I'll buy a card. Maybe two, and put cash in them for my mom and dad." I rattled on while we finished re-stacking the cards, and I knew the others were likely watching our interaction closely from different corners of the store.

"This may seem weird, but your glasses look nice on you," I offered a compliment, then rushed on with more unnecessary words. "I wish my mom wore cute glasses like that. She's always losing her reading glasses, though. We spent twenty minutes in the laundry room just yesterday searching for them."

Would my indirect mention of another mother trigger any reaction in Lydia? Any longing for her long-lost son?

Lydia smiled kindly, a faraway look crossing her face. "You remind me of someone. Full of energy and life." She blinked hard before her professional demeanor returned. "Well, let me know if you need anything else. The register is by that wall, over there."

I watched her walk briskly away, my curiosity burning brighter than before. Who had I reminded her of?

"Emma!" Harper's loud whisper made me gasp. The others suddenly surrounded me, questions filling the air.

"That was her. Did you learn anything?" Dylan asked excitedly.

"What did you say? I saw you talking to her." Jack asked.

As I recounted the odd interaction, we huddled in an empty corner of the store by the dressing rooms.

"She seemed sad when you mentioned your mom," Duke said. "I have good ears and heard it all. So maybe her motherly instincts aren't dead."

Harper nodded slowly. "Granny said she mostly keeps to herself. But even lone wolves long for a pack sometimes."

I thought back to Lydia's weary eyes and wistful half-smile. Harper was right. As cautious as we needed to be, Lydia appeared sincere, and now that she knew Mark was alive and she'd met him, maybe reviving her pack instinct to becoming a splendid mother might happen. Perhaps I'm wrong about her. Maybe she's trying to fix her relationship with Mark.

I ran up to Lydia at the counter. "Do you like taffy? I love cinnamon taffy. My dad buys it wholesale for me."

"No, thank you. I'm not much for sugary snacks."

Dylan pushed me when he walked close by and motioned for me to follow him over three aisles.

"What is it?" I asked.

Duke moved beside Dylan and said, "I know where she parked her car. I could put this tracker on it. Then we can monitor her movements."

Dylan nodded. "There's an old beat-up blue car in the alley, and we think she drives it."

Jack frowned. "I don't know, guys ..."

Sebastian waved his arms like he was about to throw a fit. "You can't do that. It's probably illegal. We can't break the law."

Duke said, "But if she's an alien. This might be necessary."

Sebastian sighed and marched out the store's front door to remove himself from our mischief.

I then urged Jack. "Your ankle keeps you from moving so fast. Maybe you should join Sebastian."

Jack wiped his nose with the back of his hand. "This cast won't slow me down. I'll be ready for track in the spring. You'll see. This won't keep me from running."

After a few minutes, we left the store with our purchases: a stuffed animal and candy canes, two greeting cards, a couple of gift cards, and some wrapping paper, and Duke and Dylan couldn't quit talking about the tracking device.

With our bags in our hands, we walked around the building and spotted Lydia loading a box into a faded blue car.

When she went inside, Dylan acted swiftly, taking the device from Duke. He attached it under her rear bumper with the ease of one who had pranked before, although I did not know how it would stay put.

Confident we were breaking the law, Sebastian raced to Lydia's car and felt for the device just as she returned to the alley. "Can I help you? That's my car. What's this about?"

Sebastian held the tracker behind his back, and I inched up behind him, took it from his hand, and stuck it into my jacket pocket. I apologized, "We're sorry. We're just nosey. Mark has a real mom now, and we can't believe it."

Harper waved from the sidewalk where she'd moved to. "Come on, guys. Hurry, we'll be late." And with that, we ran like chickens being chased by a goose, like guilty kids who, thankfully, didn't break the law.

Soon, we were a safe distance away, and I pulled out the air tag and handed it to Duke. "We're investigators. We do it the right way or not at all."

Dylan stood next to me. "That's right, Duke. What were you thinking?"

Duke argued, "You put me up to it."

"Whatever. What a waste of my time. I'm going home." Duke pounded down the sidewalk, and Dylan gave a sly grin but followed his brother.

I leaned on a pole, one with a poster of Custard, unsure what to think or do—or where we should go.

"Lydia's probably headed home now," Jack said, fidgeting nervously. "I hope she doesn't tell your mom and dad what happened."

"Don't worry. She's the one who's been missing in plain sight." I mouthed, realizing how harsh my words sounded.

Jack hobbled along, and Sebastian, Harper, and I came to the fork in the road, split by the old Methodist Church on one side and apartments on the other.

Pulling on my sleeve, Jack said, "Look, I knew this town was small, but how small—is an understatement. There's the blue car. It's just like Lydia's."

Harper raced ahead of us. "I'll check it out." She charged across the road to the parking lot and waved as we walked slower because of Jack's boot.

For the next twenty minutes, the four of us stood catching our breath, waiting outside an apartment building on the shabbier side of downtown. Lydia had parked her car on the side, but which apartment was hers?

We entered the worn lobby where mailboxes lined the wall, and people had penciled their names on the faces of each box. Apartment 2E had the name *Walsh* written on it.

Before we could decide our next move, the inside lobby door swung open—which led to the private elevator area for residents. We darted behind the nearby stairwell just as Lydia exited the doorway and went outside.

And to our shock, Mark was with her!

We watched speechlessly through the glass doors as Lydia hugged him tightly, but she quickly returned inside and headed to the elevator.

We barreled outside to Mark, and he spun around. "Guys! What are you doing here?" His smile tightened into a frown. "Did you follow me?"

Harper yelled, "No! We were walking by and saw Lydia's blue car, and you came out. We just happened this way."

The idea of a tracker suddenly felt like an anchor around my neck. "We might owe you an explanation ..." I began guiltily.

Sebastian echoed my fear. "This is not the way I expected today to go." And Jack hobbled up. "Me, neither."

Mark shook his head, his expression thoughtful rather than angry. "It's okay. I get it. You're just watching out for me."

He explained how he and my parents had finished up with the pastor and then said, "The police had given me my mother's address. Emma, your mom and dad dropped me off."

Lydia appeared from the double doors behind us. "It seems I have some spies following me around today. It's my stalker friends from the store. Mark and I are taking a ride to talk and get to know each other, and I left my keys in my apartment."

I shrugged my shoulders. "It's a small town. You run into the same people a lot," I said, knowing I'd never run into Lydia before she showed up at my house.

Lydia moved to the parking area. "I'll pull the car around and pick you up, Mark."

And with that, Mark whispered in my ear. "Lydia's apartment doesn't have any Christmas decorations. I think she's getting back on her feet."

Jack's face lit up. "That's it. Lydia needs some holiday cheer."

Mark agreed with Jack. "Lydia mentioned she gets lonely with just her two cats. What do you say we give her a proper Christmas?"

Jack applauded. "I love cats. And Christmas."

Investigating Lydia's motives consumed my free time, but to help Mark, I had to press on.

**

The following day, Duke, Dylan, Sebastian, Jack, and Harper met me at Lydia Walsh's tiny apartment, our arms loaded with gifts and holiday fixings. None of us minded delaying our festivities for a few hours. Not when there was Christmas joy to spread and hearts to lift. Besides, I could still check her out and see what she might be up to.

Duke and Dylan were a whirlwind, decking the rooms with garlands and strings of lights. Jack helped Lydia make hot chocolate while barely bumping into anything with his cast. Harper arranged her granny's homemade Christmas cookies on festive plates, and Sebastian longed to tell us the Christmas story about Jesus—a truth he wanted to share.

Mark grinned a lot, glanced at the floor even more, yet persisted in aiding Lydia in placing a felt stocking by the tree with his name on it. I even caught Lydia wiping away a few tears behind her eyeglasses.

Could Lydia Walsh have received the greatest gift in that cramped, makeshift celebration—a *pack* to call her own?

And yes, the gift went both ways. Amid the twinkling lights, chatter, and warmth, Mark hugged Lydia, perhaps with less enthusiasm than I wished to see—but this was his first Christmas without his adoptive parents.

Although everyone is in a festive mood, my elbow itching flares up whenever I approach her. I can't pinpoint the cause, but something has worsened my itching—usually. That means there's a clue to solve, or I could have a rash.

Lydia's lived secretly in Lick Skillet for how long, and now her returning as Mark's long-lost birth mother made even bigger headlines. Everything about this felt wrong.

Pam Kumpe

Duke & Dylan

THE UNRAVELING THREAD

On Christmas Eve afternoon, the air was frosty and filled with the scent of winter, accompanied by the faint jingle of bells in the distance. I witnessed a flurry of activity in Lydia's tiny apartment, yet I doubted her. However, laughter bounced off the walls as everyone pitched in to make the holiday special for Mark and Lydia.

Duke and Dylan, with their typical flair for the dramatic, had turned the living room into a winter wonderland, tinsel and strings of lights twinkling in every corner. Despite his cast, Jack was the designated hot chocolate master, stirring the pot with a concentration that made me chuckle.

Harper flitted around, arranging more cookies and ensuring everything was perfect. Mark, his eyes shining brighter than the Christmas tree, helped Lydia hang decorations, and he shared stories of his life. "I love baseball and play left field, mostly on the tournament team back in

Oklahoma. On my league team, I play pitcher and shortstop." Marks's words trailed off, the sorrow in his tone apparent by the silence as we looked at him. "I had just signed up for this year's season."

I rushed to his side. "Look, Harper's grandmother made these. They are the best sugar cookies ever. Try one."

Mark reached for the cookie, biting into it while moving to get a hot chocolate. I eavesdropped on his conversation with Jack.

"I won't get to play on my team this year," Mark said, nibbling on the cookie. "I won't ever sleep in my old bed, either. How will I get my clothes? Wait, I left my baseball glove at our lake house in Arkansas. I'll never get it back, will I? And I won't see my old friends anymore."

"I'm your friend. And we have baseball in Texas. I'm a catcher. You can play on my team. I'm also trying to get Sebastian to play, but he's not into sports." Jack said, his words trying to lighten the heaviness we all felt.

Sebastian shrugged his shoulders. "I heard you say my name, Jack, and for the tenth time, I'm not playing baseball."

Mark said, "It would be fun to play with both of you. At least, I know the two of you."

A grin landed on Sebastian's face as if he knew what it felt like to be the new kid in town—which he does—from last summer.

I ran down the hall behind Custard, who chased Lydia's cats, where I noticed two suitcases on top of her bed. "Stop! You don't have to bark at them. They'll scratch you on the nose if you catch them."

Moving back down the hallway to the living room, I wondered why Lydia had suitcases out—she couldn't be leaving with Mark. Could she?

Disregarding the worry, the unmistakable warmth in the room wove a tangible thread of joy and friendship. Even Lydia, who I had reservations about, seemed sincerely touched by Duke and Dylan's silliness and Harper's teasing of the twins.

The doorbell rang, a sharp, unexpected chime that cut through the laughter. Lydia excused herself to answer the door, wiping her hands on her apron. Curiosity pricked at me, and I followed her, lingering off to the side.

Lydia talked to a man in a sharp-fitted suit, his face grave and businesslike. "Ms. Walsh, I have some bad news," he said, and I saw Lydia stiffen slightly.

"Yes. What do you mean?" Her voice was cautious, guarded.

The man cleared his throat and glanced inside the apartment, his eyes meeting mine. I turned to straighten an ornament on the Christmas tree, and he said, "I'm here to discuss a matter of some importance. May I come in?"

Lydia hesitated for a moment before nodding, leading him into the kitchen. I pretended to straighten the skirt around the Christmas tree now, and my heart pounded, and I crept closer, trying to catch snippets of their conversation.

"It's about ... the insurance policy," the man said, his voice low and insistent. "The beneficiary, Mark McIntosh, would have received a substantial amount from the policy, but as you know, a recent change listed you as the beneficiary. There's a concern about the timing of this change, and that's where it gets sticky. Before we can make any payment, we need to clear up those irregularities."

Lydia's hands clenched at her sides, her knuckles white. "I don't understand. I was told everything was in order."

The man shook his head. "I'm afraid not, Ms. Walsh. We need to investigate further. I tried to call you but thought a visit might be better. So I'll be in touch. Or someone else with the insurance company … will contact you."

Lydia's face crumpled, a look of despair washing over her. "But I need that money," she said, her voice cracking. "I was going to use it… to leave this rotten place. I hate it here in Lick Skillet! I'm going back to California!"

The shock of what I heard hit me so hard I thought my head might explode, but I'd hit it on the wall during all her harsh words. Lydia had been counting on the life insurance money from Mark's adoptive parents, money that should have been his. And now, because of some unknown deceit, Lydia's actions raised questions about her integrity—what in the world was she up to?

The man offered a few more comments before leaving, and Lydia closed the door behind him with a shaky hand. She leaned against the door momentarily; her shoulders slumped in defeat.

My mind was a whirlwind of emotions. Anger, confusion, and a fierce protective instinct for Mark all battled for dominance. I had to tell him, to warn him about what was happening. But how could I shatter the happiness he'd found on this Christmas Eve day?

With a deep breath, I stepped back into the living room, my eyes seeking Mark, who laughed at something Duke had said, utterly carefree and content.

"Mark," I called, my voice steadier than I felt. "Can we talk? It's important."

He followed me into the hallway as Custard chased one of Lydia's cats. His expression turned tense and his lips pursed. "Emma, what's wrong? What happened?"

I looked into his eyes. "Mark, there's something you need to know about Lydia and the life insurance money from your parents' death."

I explained everything I'd overheard, and I saw the confusion, then the dawning and the despair that settled in his eyes—and the way his eyebrows slanted downward. The puzzle pieces were falling into place. Not how I wished, but the truth about Lydia's intentions seemed clear—she didn't want Mark. She wanted his money.

"But she's my birth mom," Mark said, his voice small and lost. "She wouldn't ... she couldn't do that to me, could she?"

I squeezed his hands, wishing I could shield him from this pain. "I don't know, Mark. But we need to tell my parents."

He nodded, a determined light sparking in his eyes. "You're right. But maybe you misunderstood."

I sighed. "I hope that's the case."

Together, we returned to the living room, our faces set with resolve. The festive atmosphere had dimmed slightly. A shadow of uncertainty hung low—like a bitter frost. No one should feel such a cold ache at Christmas.

Dylan and Duke, unaware of the shadow, spun in circles with tinsel wrapped around them, and Harper giggled. "Let me put a Christmas bow on each of your heads. You two are double trouble."

Jack glanced at me and asked, "You okay, Emma?"

I picked up Custard, and in a low voice, I bent closer to Jack. "Lydia's up to no good. She doesn't want Mark. She wants his life insurance money."

"That can't be true. Look at her. She's playing the part too great to be lying." Jack sucked on a candy cane. "I hope you're wrong."

One thing was sure: I was ready to stand with Mark and protect him no matter what the truth or the future brought. And if that meant uncovering deceit to find a way forward— our bond would be unbreakable.

What kind of mother would do something like this to her own son?

IDENTITY QUESTION

The festive atmosphere at Lydia's apartment had taken a sad turn, and I watched Mark, his confusion and hurt etched on his face. I tried to reconcile the loving image of a mother, the one Mark deserved, but Lydia Walsh was not that person. I wouldn't say I liked it, not one bit, but the itch on my elbow intensified, and the uncertainty gnawed at me. But truth matters. My youth pastor teaches us this, although I struggle with telling the truth myself.

"Emma, do you really think Lydia is being dishonest?" Harper whispered to me as we gathered our coats to leave, and she had a concerned look in her eyes, mirroring my feelings.

"I don't know," I admitted, my doubt, my thoughts racing. "Something feels off. I mean, why hasn't she ever tried to find Mark before now? And now, suddenly, when there's money involved ..."

Harper nodded; her brow wrinkled. "We need to find out more about her. Maybe there's something we're missing."

Dylan and Duke, who'd been eavesdropping, chimed in. "We can help," Dylan declared. "Let's do some detective work!"

Jack, nursing his third hot chocolate, raised an eyebrow. "You guys sound like you're in a spy novel. Be careful, okay? We don't want to make things worse for Mark."

"We'll be discreet," Duke said, although the mischievous glint in his eye made me wonder.

We said our goodbyes, promising to meet at the Mitchell house and not letting Mark know our plans. Outside the apartment building, we waited for Mom to pick us up. I had called her earlier, using Jack's phone, and I noticed Mark was quieter than usual, his eyes looking downward.

Mark finally spoke as we waited, kicking at the blades of dry winter grass. "Thank you for decorating Lydia's apartment. It was almost a great Christmas."

Sebastian responded, "I'm sorry, Mark. This was supposed to be a great day. I was going to tell the story of Jesus tonight, how he was born in a manger, but this day didn't go like we wanted."

Mark sighed, kicking at a pebble. "I wish Jesus would have saved me from all of this—I just want my old life back. What if Lydia only wants life insurance? I just met her, and now, this is happening."

Sebastian, wiping his nose, said, "I understand. I've missed my parents every day for almost six years," he coughed as if concealing his tears and sat on the curb.

Mark then said, with a shrill tone. "This is so hard. I miss my mom and dad. We always had breakfast at the lake house in Arkansas on Christmas morning. This Christmas feels so different without them. And now, I'm so confused about Lydia. Everything's off, and I'm suffocating."

I tried to reassure him. "I'm so sorry. The first Christmas after my little brother died was the hardest. It's still tough, but it's different. Now I remember his smile when Christmas comes."

Duke put his arm around Mark's shoulder. "Hey, my parents read the Bible story on Christmas Eve night. Maybe you could come to our house. Our dad plays the guitar and sings. What do you say?"

"I play the guitar," Mark said, his breathing getting heavier, his eyes watering. "I hadn't thought about it, but my guitar was in the trunk of our car. Now it's gone, too."

Harper said, "I can't play any instruments, but I love to sing."

I pulled on her sleeve. "No singing. You're off-key too much for me."

Harper laughed while Mark forced a smile, and I hugged Harper sideways. "You always made me feel strong when you lived here. I sure miss that."

"Emma, you're the bravest girl in town. You don't know it yet," Harper said.

As we packed into Mom's SUV, I glanced back at the apartment building, wondering about Lydia and her story.

Sitting beside me in the seat, Mark had his hands in his pockets and looked down—a thousand things must have been going through his mind, and Jack nudged me from the other side. "Is he okay?"

"I'm not sure. Mark's life is not coming together. It makes me so sad." I said in a low voice.

Harper rattled on in the front seat, talking to my mom, and the twins and Sebastian sat in the third-row seat in the back, tossing tinsel at each other while Sebastian told them to stop.

As we climbed out of the SUV at my house, Mark went inside right behind Mom. Pulling my jacket tighter around me, I told the others. "Let's dig up whatever we can on Lydia Walsh. Get online and do your searches."

Harper nodded. "I'll see if my grandparents remember anything else about her. They've lived here forever; they might know something useful."

Dylan and Duke gave each other fist bumps. "We're on it!" Dylan said, "Let's uncover the truth!"

Jack said, wiping his bangs from his forehead. "I'll see what I can learn."

We met a few hours before dark in the kitchen at the Mitchell house, where we reconvened, huddling around three iPads, using Harper's grandparents' Wi-Fi to get online. We searched for anything related to Lydia Walsh, and the minutes ticked by, each one stretching longer as we dug through online records, news articles, and social media. "I can't stay long. It's Christmas Eve, and Mom made plans for supper at seven," I said, staring at the light from my iPad.

Harper gasped, drawing our attention to her screen. "Guys, look at this," she said, pointing to an article from years back. "It's about a woman named Lydia Walsh, who people reported missing in Hemet, California," Harper said, pointing to the photo of the woman. "They never found her. They even suspect a serial killer."

We leaned in, reading the details. This Lydia Walsh had been in her early twenties when she disappeared without a trace. My heart skipped a beat. "No way. She looks just like our Lydia Walsh. Oh my goodness! Wait, the eyes are a little different, not quite the same, and the skin color is off, too. Our Lydia is dark-skinned; the one in the story is much lighter. What is going on?"

Harper let out a high-pitched sound. "But this one favors the Lydia Walsh we've met who lives here."

"But how can that be?" Jack asked, frowning. "If she's been missing for years ...?"

Dylan's eyes widened. "What if the woman we know isn't Lydia Walsh? What if she's an imposter and is pretending to be the real Lydia?"

My mind raced, and I said, "When we were at Lydia's apartment, I heard her tell the insurance man she wanted to return to California. And I saw two suitcases on her bed," I said, my heartbeat in my throat and my chin quivering.

The possibility hung in the air, heavy and threatening. It added a plot twist, which I had never expected. And now, the sudden interest in Mark and his life insurance policy made more sense.

I stopped the spiraling thoughts. "Wait, but the police said they found her. Maybe we're off on this."

Jack said, "I bet she read about Mark in the newspaper. I bet she acted on this and called them herself. Maybe she's been lurking in the background, hoping for this all along."

"We need to tell Mark," Harper said, her voice urgent. "Wait, how did you get Mark to stay behind at your house when you left? Didn't he suspect something since you were leaving without him?"

"He was busy with Custard, teaching him tricks, acting like he was fine. And then Dad showed Mark his collection of baseball cards, and I slipped off."

As we gathered our things, ready to leave the dusty house and go home with a valid clue added to our investigation, Jack's cell phone buzzed with a text.

I squinted, glancing at his phone. "Who is it?"

"Let me read it. Wait, it's from Mark."

"But when did you give Mark your phone number? And when did he get a phone?"

"I didn't. Mark must have memorized it from when he found my phone the other day. Wait, the text is coming from your mom's cell phone."

Jack turned his phone so I could read it: Tell Emma I believe her about the insurance money. I know this lady isn't my mother. I knew it from the beginning, and I'm leaving for good. Please don't come for me.

Pointing to the top of the message on the phone, I said, "Mom must have left her phone on a table or something." Then, the panic surged through me, and I yelled, "Mark's running away!"

Without another word, we rushed out of the Mitchell house, the winter air biting at our faces as we raced to find our friend.

Mark would soon be out on the streets again, somewhere alone, and it was up to us to bring him back—because no one should be alone on Christmas.

As my eyes burned with the idea, I couldn't help but feel responsible. But there was no time for guilt now; we had to find him before it was too late—before Mark left.

At my house, Mom said he left the house to meet us—all untrue. So the search stretched onward, our calls for Mark echoing through the neighborhood as cars pulled into driveways, with families gathering for the holiday.

"Will we find him?" I said, shaking my head.

Harper said, "It's getting late. When people don't want to be found, they go far away."

"So, do you think he would leave Lick Skillet?"

"I would. I would get out of town and fast."

The moon climbed higher and then lower, casting long shadows as we checked every place we could think of—the park, the alleys, even returning to the old Mitchell house three times, and returning to the fork in the road where Lydia's apartment building sat and then back by the woods. Mom and Dad checked with Lydia, but she wasn't home.

Then, as we rounded a corner near the baseball fields, Harper pointed ahead. "There! That's him!"

Sure enough, there was Mark, a figure walking briskly away from a dugout with Custard by his side. Until that moment, I didn't realize Mark had taken my dog. We called out, our voices desperate, but he didn't stop or look back. And neither did Custard.

The twins showed up, with Jack by their side, and I said, "Dylan. Duke. Go around that way! Jack, you go straight." I directed, pointing down a side street and then ahead. "We'll try to cut him off!"

Our breaths came in ragged gasps as we pushed ourselves to run faster. Mark was just ahead, but he was moving with determination, making my heart ache.

Finally, as Dylan emerged from the side street, Mark stopped, trapped between us. He looked at us, his expression a mix of defiance and despair.

"Mark, please," I said, stepping closer. "We're just trying to help."

He shook his head, his voice barely audible. "You don't understand. I can't stay here after knowing the truth. Not with *her* living here."

"We know Lydia's not your real mom," Harper blurted out. "We've discovered she's an imposter. The real Lydia Walsh has been missing for years. She most likely died in California, and this *Lydia i*s pretending to be her. They could be twins; they favor so much."

Mark's eyes widened in shock, then filled with tears. "I knew something was wrong. I ... I didn't want to believe it."

"We'll figure this out, Mark," I promised, reaching for his hand. "You have friends here."

He hesitated, then finally, slowly, took my hand. "But I just want a family," he whispered.

As we walked back to my house, the stars twinkling overhead, I knew we had an imposter to expose and a friend to protect. Once in my yard, four police cars drove up with lights flashing, and Mom and Dad stood on the porch—the seriousness of the situation growing like a parade of sorrow.

The conversation with Mom and Dad, Duke and Dylan, Harper and Sebastian, and Jack and I took place simultaneously, and then Jane appeared in my front yard with a flashlight. "What's going on? I heard sirens."

I assured her. "It's fine, Jane. Just fine."

"It doesn't seem fine." Jane inched closer as if she had to see more—and then she stood in front of Mark, lifting his chin, and said, "You look like your mother. Just like her. She was fair like you, and you have her eyes."

Mark stepped back, as if that was too much to take in—and ran into the house, slamming the door.

But then, after minutes of explaining and with police officers leaving, we went inside, and the back door leading to the backyard was wide open—Mark followed through on his desire to leave. I ran to the porch. "No! Mark, you can't leave," I said and turned to find Custard tied to the fence with his leash, whining.

I rushed to the middle of my road, crying as Jane moved to my side. "What now?"

"Mark's gone! He's run away again!" My words faded into the darkness, and I swallowed so hard I choked. *Was Mark seriously gone this time?*

Pam Kumpe

Mark McIntosh

TRIP TO THE LAKE

Mark vanished into the unknown, and ten excruciatingly long days passed by. The arrest of our local Lydia Walsh, or whoever she was, brought no comfort, only more questions, and a deepening sense of loss. Custard, once a bundle of joy and energy, now lay listlessly by the door, his sad whines filling our quiet house.

Harper's text messages were the only thread of hope I clung to, as I'd gotten my first cell phone on Christmas morning—not that I even enjoyed having a phone that much with all the sadness. But the investigation wasn't over. We had to find Mark.

With Harper's online searches, she'd found Mark's family lake house in Hot Springs, Arkansas, the one now listed for sale, most likely empty and dark. Convincing my parents to let me spend the weekend with Harper was easy, given the circumstances—they knew how upset I was after Mark's disappearance. Besides, Harper and I felt an itch to check out the lake house.

"Mom, I promise to listen to Harper's mom. I will say thank you. I won't stay up too late. I have my coat. And my cell. Yes, I'll be good." I assured my mom, hoping my words meant the truth, but the truth of the matter is I may need forgiveness after this weekend.

Dad reached for my shoulders, one hand on each. "You're my girl. Watch that water. You know you can't swim."

"I will be careful. Harper's not fond of water either, but she can swim."

My parents understood the need for me to be with my friend during this challenging time, unaware of my true intention to search for Mark.

I packed lightly; worry was far heavier than anything in my backpack. Custard perked up slightly as I prepared to leave, sensing the change in routine. "You're coming with me, boy," I whispered, stroking his head. "Maybe we'll find Mark, huh?"

My mom met Harper's mom halfway between our towns down the interstate, an hour for each of us. I loaded up with Harper in the back seat at a gas station, waving to my mom.

"Harper, this is great. We must check out your lead. Mark must be somewhere." She shushed me. "Don't talk so loudly. My mom has ears like a hawk."

"Did you two say something?" She asked, holding the steering wheel.

"No, we're good. Just catching up," Harper said, her smile telling me to watch what I said.

The trip to Hot Springs flew by, and plans, clues, and thoughts of Mark consumed Harper and me and what awaited for us at the lake house.

"If he's there, we'll find him, Emma," Harper said, her voice steady and low. "We have to."

**

Since it was Friday night, the time got away, especially since Harper's mom dished out spaghetti, garlic toast, and chocolate pie when we got to their house—and she had her heart set on watching a family movie together.

So Harper and I got up early in the morning. Besides, Custard was showing out by rolling over and barking too much. But he could shake your hand now—a trick Mark had taught him.

Thankfully, Harper lived in a nearby cove, not far away from Mark's old summer home, but as it got later, he sensed our unrest; Custard stayed close, his presence a silent comfort.

"Harper, I hope you don't mind. Custard likes to sleep with me."

"No, I don't mind. But my cat, Taffy, might."

"When did you name your cat Taffy? I thought his name was Pinecone."

"When we moved here, he ate all the cinnamon taffy you'd given me, and I changed his name to Taffy."

"I love it. What a glorious name."

"This way, I'll never forget you, my best friend."

Then, suddenly, Taffy shot into the bedroom, only for Custard to chase the white cat down the hallway and back—

154

then returning, and he finally launched with all paws into bed with us, ready to sleep.

"I'm sorry. I don't think Custard likes your cat or will share the bed."

Harper giggled. "I'm not sure Taffy is a fan of Custard, either."

I stretched out, fluffed my pillow, and nestled under the covers. "Night, the adventure awaits tomorrow."

In seconds, Taffy hissed from the floor beside the bed and jumped onto Harper's pillow while Custard let out a low growl under his breath.

**

Yawning, I sat up, glanced out the window at the lake, and saw the morning sun casting a soft glow over the water. Custard and Taffy were curled up together—maybe they would become best friends, too. After breakfast, Harper and I told her mom we were taking a trail hike along the waterfront, and so we headed out, the journey filled with anxious anticipation. I clipped the leash to Custard's collar to ensure he didn't get away from us.

"The house is across the cove from us, not too far down the trail," Harper said.

"I can't wait. Wouldn't that be great if Mark's hiding there?" I asked, unsure if that was even possible.

"I would love for that to be true, but let's not get our hopes up."

Custard padded along between us, his head bouncing, his nose sniffing as if he, too, understood the importance of what we were about to do.

Soon, we stood across the water from the lake house where Mark had once spent his summers. It was a lonely spot against the backdrop of serene waters, its windows staring out like empty eyes. It was a beautiful place, though, secluded and peaceful, opposite the turmoil I felt inside. The stairs to the hilltop were longer than the walk to the old Mitchell house— or so it seemed.

"How will we get across?"

"I have our canoe tied up at the bank, right over there. We'll take it across the water."

I sighed. "I'm not fond of water."

"It's fine. The water's not deep in the cove. It's just wet." She laughed, tugging on my arm.

After we loaded into the canoe and Custard barked at the flyover of the geese, we paddled across. "Wow! That's a lot of stairs," I said, glancing up.

As we stood on the dock, facing an incline, Harper said, "It's normal here. Hills and valleys. Twists and turns. And stairs."

"That describes life—hills and valleys and twists and turns."

Harper said, "You're always such a deep thinker."

We both laughed, and I wished for a second that I was more athletic, like Jack. "This will take forever!"

"Many of the docks in our area take you up long, winding staircases to the houses at the top of the hills," Harper said.

We climbed for what seemed like forever, and Custard had to be carried the last half, too many steps for his tiny legs. I wondered what we might find inside and reached for the handle. "It's unlocked," I said, swinging one of the four glass doors open with a gentle push. The inside was as quiet as the world outside, the air thick with the dust of abandonment.

"We'll start upstairs," Harper said in the stillness.

We went upstairs, the open ceiling area letting in light from the enormous windows on the second floor, and we moved through the house, checking each room, and I held my breath. We found nothing in the first two bedrooms, just furniture and layers of dust.

Then, we reached what must have been Mark's room; with the navy bedspread and baseball glove on the dresser, Custard suddenly sprang to life. He pawed at trash and old plates of food on the floor by the bed, and then he dug at a piece of wood by the wall.

"What is it, Custard?" I asked, kneeling to examine where the wooden plank bounced off. Inside the spot was a green cigar box—hidden away—that must have been important to Mark.

I opened it, my heart pounding with anticipation. "Harper, look. There's a yo-yo, a baseball card, the dog charm Mark had worn around his neck—and a small notebook."

As I read, sitting there on the floor, the diary held the deepest secrets of Mark's heart. "Harper, this is so sad. He's written about how no one wants him, how he doesn't fit in."

Tears filled my eyes, the words a stark reminder of the friend we'd lost. Custard whined softly, nuzzling the box as if he, too, could feel Mark's presence.

"We have to find him, Harper," I said, thick with emotion. "We must let him know we care about him."

Harper nodded, wiping away a tear. "He's been here, or that charm wouldn't be in the box. We'll find him and bring him home."

"But whose home? Where does he belong?" I asked, the heaviness of not belonging to a family and Mark losing his adoptive parents sadder than sad.

We left the lake house with heavy hearts, no sign of Mark, except for the box of Mark's memories and his baseball glove, which I took—a treasure to return to him one day.

The small diary had many blank pages, meaning Mark's story wasn't over, and oddly enough, he journaled in the same way his biological grandmother, Joyce, did—a trait she'd passed on to him.

Custard seemed more determined than ever, leading the way down the wooden steps to the trail with a newfound sense of purpose, and we paddled across the cove in the canoe.

As we walked down the winding trail back to Harper's house, the journey was quiet, each of us lost in our thoughts. But as we approached Harper's home, a figure emerged from the bushes on the trail, a familiar silhouette that made my heart leap.

"Mark!" I cried, leaping at him like a long-lost sister.

He stood there frozen, his hair wild and unkempt, hesitant and weary, but it was him. Alive and unharmed.

"Emma. Harper. I'm sorry," he said, his voice barely a whisper. "I just ... I needed to figure things out on my own," Mark said, his words shaking. "And by the way, how did you two find me?"

"I should be the one asking the questions." I circled him. "How did you end up here? You're two hours from Lick Skillet. Why do you keep running away? What do you expect to find?"

Harper put her hand over my mouth. "Stop interrogating him. That's why he leaves. Too much pressure from everyone!" Pushing her off, I said, "I'm sorry. Mark. I was so worried."

Mark pointed. "Is that my glove?" He snatched it. "So you've been to my house?"

"Yes, we came searching for you. I knew that if I carried your glove, I'd find you. And here you are," I said, the tears dropping like rain.

Mark took a big breath. "The night I left, I was so afraid of being placed somewhere—somewhere with more new people. So I ran. And I rode with a truck driver and told him I was going home. He must have believed me because he gave me a ride."

"That trucker could have killed you. You know that, don't you?" I said, taking his glove from him and hitting him with it.

"Stop hitting me," Mark said, grabbing the glove from my hand as Custard licked Mark's shoe.

Harper scolded Mark. "What were you thinking?"

Mark chuckled. "Oh, it's not like you two have permission to look for me, do you?"

Harper slugged him. "That's not the same as running away. We're going back to my house. You can't live like this."

"Well, I'm fine. I've been hiding at the lake house and getting food from the trash bins at that barbecue place. They throw away good food."

I yelled. "You're twelve. You can't live like this."

"I am living like this. No one misses me."

"I miss you. That's why I'm visiting Harper. She's great at research and nosier than me. She found your parent's lake house, and we came looking for you."

"Seriously, let me be."

"No! Friends go after friends," I said, wiping the tear that leaked from my eye. Harper and I enveloped him in a group hug, our tears mingling in a beautiful, slobbery mess. "You're not alone, Mark," I said, holding him tight. "You never were. We're here for you."

And as we stood there, the three of us and Custard, I knew our journey wasn't over. "Come back to Lick Skillet with me. Mom and Dad will let you stay with us as long as needed. Please?"

Harper punched his arm. "If you keep running away, you will end up in serious trouble and get taken away for good.

You must stay put and give Emma's parents a chance to help you. You can't run off like this. Never do it again."

"I don't know if I can. I don't know where I belong."

I frowned at Harper. "Fewer words, right now. Less scolding. We need a plan. And it better be a good one."

Harper sucked in the damp air as if she might spit. "Wait, my Sunday school teacher told us that our help comes from the Lord. Maybe we should ask God for His help."

Mark sniffled. "Where was God when my parents died in the accident? Or when I was born, and my real mom ran away and left me?"

I kicked at the loose sand by the water's edge. "Mark, I remember when my baby brother fell from our treehouse. My mom said Jesus held my brother as he went to heaven. I didn't want Jesus to have him, but if Brett could be anywhere— besides here, being with Jesus would be my first pick. And then my dad reminded me life is hard and that we find our hope in God."

Harper touched my shoulder. "Why don't we each say a prayer?"

"I haven't prayed in a long time," Mark said, and he wiggled like a worm in his not-so-clean clothes, tossing an odor of sweat, dirt, and rotten banana pudding my way, making my nose hair tingle.

I changed the subject. "What is all over your clothes?"

"Sorry, my last search for food put me right into a pile of desserts, and the gooey stuff stuck to my jeans."

Custard licked Mark's pant leg as if he tasted the best dessert ever. I scooted Custard aside. "Don't lick. That's nasty."

I grabbed Mark's hand, confident I'd need hand sanitizer after the prayer. "I'll pray. I'm not great at it, but we need help."

Mark moaned. "Help doesn't come my way. I get the leftovers and the trash."

I argued, "Seriously, I'm your help right now. And Harper. We keep showing up. I've never quit looking for you. I'm here now. That's help!" My yelling sent Custard into a spin, and he barked as if he agreed.

Harper added her two cents. "And we're the help you should be grateful for—Emma's a persistent and pesky friend but loyal. And I'm great at being a friend, too." Harper squeezed my hand. "Mark, you'll see. You're in a stinky place, but soon, something good will happen."

I nodded. "That's right. Bad stuff happens, but so does good."

Mark twisted his neck like an owl, rotating his head as he might take off. "Emma, I'm not sure praying will solve anything. I'm all alone. If I return with you to Lick Skillet, I'll never see either of you again. Someone will come and take me away."

"You can't live like this. You're a kid. Kids need homes. And beds. And a kitchen where you can find good food," I reminded Mark.

Mark pulled his hand away and petted Custard. "I'm eating. I have a bed. The kitchen at our lake house doesn't have food, but I'm not starving."

"You're going to get sick eating out of the trash bins. Harper and I can't fix this, but God can."

Harper giggled. "I'm praying God lets you take a bath first—and that we find you some clean clothes."

Custard gnawed on the bottom leg of Mark's pants, and I picked up my dog. "Mark, I can't believe Custard thinks your jeans are yummy."

"You get used to things when … when you're alone, when you don't have a choice." Mark wiped his nose, then his eyes with both hands, streaks of dirt and tears mixing on his face.

Swallowing hard, I tried to encourage Mark. "You have a choice. You can come with us. Or stay here and starve!"

I gasped, praying and hoping that Mark would come with us because the help Mark needed was beyond my grasp.

THE GATE TO HOME

Two weeks ago, Harper's mom loaded us into their SUV and drove Mark, stinky clothes, and all, along with me and Custard and Harper, down the same highway that took Mark's parents in the fiery crash.

Now, with the first winter snow at the end of January, a sight we often never see here, we've gathered at my house for pizza for a celebration no one saw coming, another story that will go down in history in Lick Skillet.

Jane, my neighbor who chatted with me over the fence, is why Lick Skillet is alive with excitement and plenty of news teams. They're covering a story about a boy who survived a fiery wreck, who hid at the Michell house, who got rescued, who ran off, and who is now being adopted by a resident.

As I stood in my kitchen, I glanced around the room. The twins, Duke and Dylan, were there, and so were Jack and Sebastian and Mom and Dad, and of course, Harper came to town for Mark's party.

My heart tugged with heaviness for Mark at losing his adoptive parents, yet the emotion of happiness rose with the idea of his having a home.

Custard, the unassuming hero of our tale, kept running over and laying his head at Mark's feet, symbolizing the silent strength that guided us to this moment.

Jane Hendershot, once just a nosey neighbor, had revealed a bond that tied her deeply to Mark's past as a longtime friend of Joyce Mitchell, and she wanted to do this act of courage to honor her late friend—to love the grandchild Joyce never knew—fully.

"Mark, life has a way of bringing us full circle," Jane said, her voice soft with a warmth that felt like an embrace—her words wrapping around my heart like a breeze of hope.

I moved closer to Jane and said, "When I first saw you in the photos with Joyce, I never expected this—that you would adopt Mark."

"I've known Mark's grandparents since we were all children playing in each other's backyards. Joyce and Melvin would be so proud to know that Mark had found a new beginning and that he'd live in Lick Skillet and be raised in such a significant community that's so close knit," Jane said, smiling.

Mark looked from Jane to me and then petted Custard, his eyes glistening. "I ... I don't know what to say. I've felt so lost," he admitted, his voice whispering. "But now, I'm finding pieces of a new family."

I reached out, squeezing Mark's hand. "You're not just finding pieces. You're receiving a whole new set of friends, too. And you'll always have me to pester you. And Custard."

Mark added, a small smile breaking through as he looked down at my dog. "Custard seems to like me."

Jack, nursing his broken ankle but ever the great friend, said, "Emma, you need to have your dad install a gate in the chain-link fence between Ms. Jane's backyard and yours. That would help Custard so he could visit back and forth."

Sebastian nodded, his usual reserve giving way to a softness in his eyes. "It's more than just Custard visiting. It's about keeping doors open. To family, to friends, to whatever the future holds. Custard thinks he belongs to both of you."

The twins, Dylan and Duke, usually the first to crack a joke, were unusually solemn. "We're all part of this story now," Dylan said. "It's like we're all getting a new beginning."

Duke looked around the group, his gaze lingering on Mark and Custard. "Yeah, and we've got the best guardian angel a bunch of kids could ask for," he said, nodding at Custard, who wagged his tail as if in agreement.

As plans were discussed, laughter and chatter filled the room, and Mark stole glances at the faces of his new family. His eyes sparkled like a sunrise on a perfect day, and I couldn't believe Mark's forever found sat next door to me.

**

The following day, Dad, Mom, Jane, Mark, and I gathered in the backyard to select a spot where the new gate would connect our lives even more closely.

"You know," Jane said, "this is just the first of many adventures ahead."

Mark nodded. "I'm ready for them. All of them. With Custard and with you, Ms. Jane." He scooted close to Jane, and she placed her arm around his shoulders. They gazed at each other like life had answered a prayer—like joy coming in the morning.

Custard bounced between Mark and me in the shallow blanket of snow, looking up at us, wagging his tail, and slinging snowflakes. His presence was a reminder of the mysterious ways seasons can bring hearts together, heal, and unite.

No one ever called to claim Custard—which only meant the mystery would remain—which was fine with me. Or maybe God sent Custard to rescue all of us.

In Lick Skillet, under the vast Texas sky, a new family was born, not of blood but of boundless love and the not-so-angelic dog who knew where he was most needed. "Custard, stop digging at the bottom of the fence. You'll have a gate soon enough," I hollered.

But it was too late. The tunnel in the ground beneath the chain-link fence—meant we didn't need a gate because when you have paws like Custard, you dig your way to where you want to go.

Then Jane, who had reappeared after disappearing inside my house for a minute, returned with her guitar and handed it to Mark. "This belonged to your mother, the real, wonderful, and precious Lydia Walsh. She loved to play, and so did I."

Mark reached for the instrument. "This belonged to my mother?" He held the guitar close like a treasure worth millions of dollars and wept like he might never stop.

"Yes, she filled life with music. I've heard through a reliable source that you, too, know how to play."

That's when Mark cut his eyes my way—and he smiled a genuine, wide grin, more significant than a lake house or a two-story old home. And it's as if hope rose from the ashes of a December crash and landed in a January snowfall in my backyard.

Mark strummed a tune, not a song I knew, but one that required Custard's participation for a duet as he howled into the cold air. Mark's musical notes and Custard's shrieks confirmed the finding of a lost dog and boy! I hope Mark and Jane have plenty of laundry detergent—because Custard will, at some point, land on one of their beds with his muddy paws!

Custard & Emma

MORE ANIMALS TO COME

Mark jumped into the school scene this week just in time for our upcoming epic field trip. We'll take a two-hour bus ride to the zoo, and 6th to 8th-grade students will go together on two buses. Yep, that includes Mark, stationed right across the hall from me in seventh grade, while the notorious twins, Duke and Dylan, hold down the corridor in eighth.

Meanwhile, Jack, Sebastian, and I are navigating sixth grade—and with tutoring from Mark and Sebastian, I'm determined to conquer math and history and not repeat this grade! If Harper were here, life would be perfect.

Recently, my nights have become much cozier after Custard returned home from staying with Mark for a while. Much to my delight, he's decided my feet are his favorite pillow. Besides, Custard's quietness is a welcome relief from the nighttime serenades of guitar strums and his howls.

Rest is crucial for me, after all. I've got big dreams of leading an investigation team one day. Sure, it'll take work, but I'm up for the challenge.

Two days ago, we witnessed something special, too. Jane and Mark were chilling on her porch in the backyard with Mark playing the guitar when a yellow dog with black-dotted ears appeared out of nowhere, barking his heart out by the fence. His name? Goose. Even though he was thin, with his ribs showing, Goose's overjoyed expression revealed his excitement upon seeing Mark.

Goose has joined Mark's band, too, as this dog can outdo Custard with his long notes. Even the neighbor, who is nearly deaf and lives two houses down from us, yells at Goose to be quiet!

Who knew our little corner of the world could hold so much music and howls and that I'd need earplugs to get any sleep? And who knew that I would need tutoring to pass sixth grade?

I will make it to the seventh grade thanks to Mark and Sebastian, who've sparked my love for history and math. After all, I'm attending college with Harper one day!

Books by Pam Kumpe

Annie Grace Kree Chronicles Series
1 Untied Shoelace
2 Unknown Soul
3 Rescue of Undaunted Spirit
4 Unwanted Sidekick
5 Unwavering Hope
6 Unshackled Courage

Other Novels
Rescue at Three Sisters Springs
Looking for Daddy's Girl
Summertime Sprinkler

Devotional
Looking for Daddy's Girl Devotional
See You in the Funny Papers
A Scoop of Inspiration

Children
In the Lick of Time
A Goat with a Tote
Hattie Holmes Holds Her Breath
Hattie and Mattie! Oh, They Love the Bunny!
Cranky Camel and the Candy Cane Caper
Cranky, the Camel, and Max Go to School
Cranky, the Camel, and Barnyard's Got Talent

Rehab Ministry
Things I Learned in Jail
From Court to Christ

Homeless Ministry
My View from the Bridge
My View from the Street
My View of the Heart

You Are Lost Series
Book One: The Mystery of Sneaky Pants
Book Two: The Mystery of Sneaky Paws
And more…

www.pamkumpe.com

Pam Kumpe

SPRING 2025

EMMA HOBBIT:
YOU ARE LOST SERIES / BOOK THREE

THE MYSTERY OF THE SNEAKY PARROTS

Duke and Dylan inherit twin parrots from their late uncle right before the school field trip to the zoo.